THE GUARDIAN'S TRUTH

CELTIC CURSES

BOOK FOUR

L.M. HATCHELL

For Krista. Thank you for being the sounding board I needed to see it through!

I stared at the television screen, my brow scrunched in confusion as I read the headline scrolling across the bottom for the third time:

Government in chaos. Emergency election called. New government expected to be elected in a matter of weeks.

When Teagan had called me in Lakeview and told me I had to come home immediately, this turn of events hadn't even factored on my radar of possible problems. So, to be sitting here, staring at Declan Bannon's smug face on the screen as he stood proudly behind a podium and declared his intention to run for Taoiseach was a little surreal.

My raven-haired best friend sat on the sofa to my left, her expression grim as she, too, stared at the screen in silence. Pete, my ex-boyfriend, appeared marginally more relaxed as he leaned against the wall closest to us, hands in his jeans pockets, but I wasn't fooled. Even just seeing the head of the Order's face again made me want to punch something. While my friends might not have felt quite so passionately, I knew they definitely weren't happy about this current development.

"I don't get it. What could he be hoping to achieve?" I looked at them both as if they could magically produce an answer that would allow this to make sense.

"Power," Pete answered simply as he pushed away from the wall. "Same thing he's always wanted."

"Yes, but political power? How does that help if he's intending to Claim magic? I don't even know if the government is aware of magic at this stage."

"That's the point though, isn't it? If the Order can set themselves up in a position of power politically, they'll be able to control the narrative when awareness of magic eventually becomes more widespread. Assuming they let it become known, that is."

A shiver ran through me as I considered this.

Up until now, the public had remained largely oblivious to the return of magic. I had no doubt many people had experienced its effects and brushed it off with some bizarrely logical explanation as humans were wont to do. The Watchers of Danu were also working to intercept any issues before they could attract media attention – something that would soon be my problem if they had their way. But eventually the magic would return in its entirety, and there would be no more sweeping it under the carpet. I didn't want to know what that future would look like with the Order driving the narrative.

Clearly having had enough, Teagan reached for the remote control and switched off the TV with a jab of her finger. "I guess now we know why they've been quiet since the night they took the cauldron."

We'd all been on edge waiting to see what Bannon would do with the magic that had been siphoned into Dagda's cauldron – my magic as well as Dub's and Carmen's. It had taken only a few days for my magic to begin replenishing, but the strange void that I'd felt in the pit of my stomach during that short time had been a horrendous reminder that at any point, Bannon could use my magic to further his cause.

Strangely, despite his newfound access to magic, Bannon and the Order seemed to disappear off the radar completely after that night. Their headquarters was looking worse for wear following Carmen's visit, and my attempts to contact Bres had been met with silence. For them to resurface now, topping the polls as the most likely party to win the upcoming election – despite not having been prominent figures in government prior to this – was suspicious at best.

I sighed and let my head fall back against the cushions of the sofa as I massaged the bridge of my nose. "I'm so sick and tired of always being on the back foot. We need to figure out what they're up to and get that damn cauldron back before they can use it."

Teagan reached over and squeezed my hand. "We'll figure it out. I've an appointment to see some pretty old texts on Celtic mythology in the city archives later today. I doubt there'll be anything about the Claiming in them, but there might be something that will help point the way."

I gave her a weak smile, as the reminder of the Claiming sent a flutter of unease through me. We still hadn't found anything more on it, other than the single reference in the book my ancestors had left me. Part of me wanted it to stay that way, but ignorance had brought me nothing but trouble up to this point. If we knew the details of the ritual, we could at least work to prevent the Order from completing it.

"You're still keeping an eye on my mam?" I asked Pete.

He nodded, his brown eyes steady and reassuring as they met my gaze. "Don't worry. I've been checking in on her whenever I can get away from the Watchers. There's been no sign of anything strange, and my wolf hasn't sensed anything either."

The tightness in my chest eased only marginally. I knew Pete would do everything he could to help keep my mam safe, but Bres's previous warning about the Order using people I cared about against me still echoed repeatedly in my head. Teagan and Pete were as capable of protecting themselves as I was – not like that said much – but my family was ignorant to all of this.

I pushed the thought firmly from my mind. We were taking precautions, and if Bannon dared to come for anyone I cared about, he'd have a werewolf, a banshee, and me to deal with.

"What about the Watchers?" I asked. "Have they said anything about this new move by the Order?"

Pete grimaced. "Brian is still pretty pissed at us for keeping him in the dark about the whole Dub and Carmen thing. He's refusing to talk to me other than to bark the occasional order to make sure I remember he's the boss. You two are going to have to show your faces at HQ soon, or he's going to follow through on his threat."

Oh yeah, his threat to have us arrested over the two unconscious bodies we'd asked him to make disappear for us.

Of course, he knew as well as we did that said bodies belonged to two ancient homicidal magical beings – one of whom was technically dead already. But it was a convenient excuse to get us to fall into line with the Watchers and their agenda. Now that Teagan was no longer making herself available for their "training" sessions, they were clearly worried that their hooks weren't buried in us deeply enough.

"Does he know I'm back yet?" I asked.

Teagan had spun a lie about a sick grandmother in order to look into a lead she'd gotten from my ancestor's book about her heritage. Since it wasn't out of the realm of belief that I'd want to support my best friend, I'd told Brian I was going with her. Instead, I'd taken a few days after my magic finally recovered to head down the country in an attempt to clear my head. Our little fib had bought us some time before we had to face up to the whole Dub and Carmen aftermath, but Brian had only allowed the few day's grace on the condition that I accept his stupid job as PR representative for the Watchers.

"Not –" Pete's phone buzzed, cutting him off mid-sentence. He looked down at it, and his eyes widened in surprise. "Actually, make that a yes. He's just messaged to say he wants to see the three of us straight away."

We all looked at each other, then looked around the room warily. I had no doubt my friends were wondering, just as I was, if Teagan's apartment had somehow been bugged. Bloody Big Brother!

Pete blew a strand of his floppy dark hair out of his eyes and moved towards the door. "I'll head in and find out what he wants. You two get settled and do what you need to. I'll hold him off as long as I can, but remember, we might still need the Watchers before this is all over. So, let's not piss him off too much, yeah?"

I groaned, but Teagan gave Pete a thin-lipped nod of acknowledgement. His eyes sparkled with amusement as he slipped out of the apartment to help delay the lecture that was no doubt coming our way.

"I suppose we were lucky to avoid him this long." I sighed and dropped my head in my hands. "He's going to make me call him Boss, isn't he."

Teagan sniggered, and I couldn't help but join her. It was either laugh or cry at this stage.

Sitting up straight, I squared my shoulders and made the decision there and then to face whatever shit was coming head-on. Pete was right; we'd likely need the Watchers on our side if we were to have a chance of getting ahead of the Order. So, I could play nice. For now, at least. But there was something I needed to do first. There was one person I could think of who might know what the Order was up, and I intended to make them talk.

"We don't have long," I said, turning to Teagan. "Bring me up to speed. Did you find anything? Who did the name belong to?"

Teagan had been off the grid for the best part of a week trying to learn more about the nature of her banshee abilities. My ancestor's book had given her some guidance while she was helping me research barrier spells, but it had been unhelpfully vague, and I had no idea if the name it provided had led Teagan on anything other than a wild goose chase.

Teagan stood and headed for the kitchen, flicking on the kettle without even checking if there was water in it. She realised her mistake a moment later and flicked it back off before filling it with water and setting it to boil once more.

"They're dead," she said, staring at the countertop, hands splayed on the smooth surface. "It seems Eliza-beth was my great-great, who knows how many greats, grandmother. She died a long time ago."

My heart sank. "Oh, Teagan. I'm sorry."

She looked up, and something like a wary hope

brightened her blue eyes. "I did find my great-grand-mother though. Anthea." Her expression hardened. "She's been alive this whole time, and my mother never told me about her."

The kettle whistled, and Teagan slammed her mug down on the counter so hard I expected it to shatter. "Tea?"

I shook my head wordlessly and waited for her to sort through her thoughts.

"It seems my heritage wasn't quite as lost as yours was," she continued finally. "My ancestors passed stories down through the generations. They were told as bedtime stories really, but even with magic gone, some of the women in my family retained a degree of premonition. My grandmother thought this was all nuts and disowned my great-grandmother when she tried to pass the stories down to my mother."

I whistled low. I knew Teagan's family was a piece of work, but to disown your mother for passing on what you believed to be a stupid story? I could see now where Teagan's mam got her shining personality from.

"What was she like? Your great-grandmother?"

Teagan's expression brightened. "You'll find out for yourself. She's coming here to meet you."

"Me?"

"Well, she's coming to meet the Guardian, but I told her you were the best I could do."

I flung a cushion at my friend, laughing. "Well, I hope she's a damn sight nicer than you."

A glance at the clock on the wall told me it was

almost noon, and I needed to get moving if I was going to do what I needed to do and make it to the Watchers HQ to appease Brian.

I stood. "Can you cover for me with the Watchers for a bit? I'll be along as soon as I can."

Suspicion narrowed Teagan's eyes. "Why? Where will you be?"

"I need to go see Bres."

CHAPTER TWO

I rapped on the door, the sound echoing through the empty hallway as my glare dared the door to remain shut. To my surprise, it didn't.

A muffled sound came from the other side and a moment later, the door swung open to reveal Bres in a pair of low-slung jeans and a white rumpled T-shirt that looked like it had been slept in. Mottled purple bruises ran from his left eye down along his jawline, and I couldn't help but notice that he kept his right arm cradled gingerly against his side as he leaned his weight against the door frame.

"I've been wondering when you'd show up." He turned to head back into the penthouse apartment, not waiting to see if I'd follow.

I gaped after him, every word of the speech I'd rehearsed on my way here dying on the tip of my tongue, along with some of my anger. What the hell had happened to him? When he hadn't returned my calls or answered the door on my previous visits, I'd assumed he was avoiding me – rightly so, after betraying us to the Order. But seeing him like this now, doubt began to creep in.

Irritation bubbled up inside me, driven by the confused thoughts warring within me. I grasped for it with both hands. Bres didn't deserve my sympathy. He'd made his choices in life, and those choices came with repercussions. I was here to find out where Dagda's cauldron was, nothing more.

Keeping that thought fixed firmly in my mind, I stormed into the apartment after him, closing the door behind me. I followed him to the living room and, in response to his raised eyebrow, sat stiffly on the soft beige sofa that faced the panoramic view of Dublin's city skylines. Bres lowered himself into his usual chair across from me, unable to hide a wince as he did. He waited in silence for me to speak.

"Why?"

The word hung in the air between us. It covered a myriad of questions I could ask, but we both knew what I meant. Still, Bres wasn't going to make it that easy.

"Why what? Why does the sun rise every morning? Why am I so damn irresistible that it's a battle not to come over here and rip off my clothes?"

I glared. "Why did you lead the Order to us? You say you want my help to stop them, yet all you seem to be doing is gathering power for them so they can complete the Claiming. Or was that your plan all along? You did say you want the Claiming to go ahead."

Bres stiffened ever so slightly at my words, but he held my gaze, unflinching. "No. It wasn't my plan. Smith & Mercer notified Bannon of the communication I sent to Dub. He'd have gotten the cauldron one way or the other. It made more sense for me to play along and claim I'd set the whole thing up. At least that way I could be there to make sure you didn't get hurt."

I sneered, doing my best to ignore the warm feeling that filled me at his concern. "You've already told me the Order needs me alive."

"You, yes. Your friends, not so much. Besides, there are a lot of ways to hurt someone."

At his soft-spoken words, my thoughts flashed to the records he'd kept on the Order. I'd only managed to photograph less than half the pages, but I'd read enough in them to know he was speaking from personal experience. The anger within me dulled once more.

"Where's the cauldron now?"

Bres gave a humourless laugh and ran his hand through his messy blond hair. "With Bannon, I should imagine. It seems Carmen did a number on the HQ, so all the important artefacts have been moved."

"To where?" I leaned forward, my tone beseeching as I silently willed him to prove me wrong, to help me with this. But his responding sigh was filled with exhaustion, and I knew I'd be disappointed.

"I don't know. I'm not privy to the Order's new location."

I frowned. "Why not?"

He looked away, refusing to meet my questioning gaze as he kept stubbornly silent.

For the first time, I stopped to truly consider his appearance. It was clear from the bruising around his face he'd been badly hurt, but how recently? The nasty purple discolouration faded out to a greenish tinge at the edges, but did that mean it was fresh or it was healing? I couldn't remember much from the first aid training I'd done during my teenage years.

"Did the Order do this to you?" I pressed, indicating his face and the arm he still held close to his side.

Bres's jaw clenched, and he still refused to look at me as he nodded.

My throat tightened, but I swallowed with effort and reminded myself yet again that what happened to Bres was not my concern. I was here for the cauldron, nothing more.

"Why?" The question slipped out even as I was silently lecturing myself on all the reasons why this was not my problem. "You led Bannon straight to us and handed him a fully charged magical weapon on a gold platter. What possible reason could they have for doing this to you?"

For the longest time, I thought he wasn't going to answer. Then he turned to look at me, and the emotion that blazed in his blue eyes almost took my breath away.

"They wanted me to bring you in. I refused. Bannon took exception to that."

My mouth dropped open, and I suddenly found my brain had lost the ability to form coherent thought. They did this to him because of me?

Sickening horror filled me. I reached desperately for the anger that had been my armour coming here, but found it slipping through my fingers like sand. The idea of him – of anyone – being hurt like this because of me was just too horrible to even consider. It didn't matter that he'd allowed Bannon to take my magic, or hell, even that he'd tricked me into starting this whole thing in the first place. I didn't want this for him.

"If the Order wanted me so badly, why didn't they just take me that night?" I said. my voice little more than a whisper. "They had guns. It's not like I could have argued."

"They couldn't risk it. Not while Teagan was there. Bannon hasn't gotten where he is by being stupid. He won't go toe-to-toe with a banshee unless he has a sure-fire way to protect himself."

I slumped back into the sofa, processing that with a numb sense of detachment. Yes, the Order had taken my magic when they'd taken the cauldron, but I was lucky that was all they'd taken. It was a sobering thought.

"Okay, then why didn't he send someone for me

after you refused?" I was *not* going to examine that part in too much detail.

Bres shrugged. "I can only guess he got sidetracked with whatever power play he's working on with the run for government. Either that, or he wasn't really in a rush to bring you in. He just wanted to test me. Make no mistake, though – he will come for you when he's ready, and he won't care who he hurts to make you comply."

I opened my mouth to tell him Bannon wouldn't be getting near anyone I cared about – then shut it without saying anything. The less Bres knew about what I was doing, the better. Instead, I looked at him, at the physical injuries still so apparent, at the shadows that haunted his blue eyes if you dared to look beyond the teasing sparkle, at the beautiful apartment that was all but devoid of personality and warmth.

"Is your revenge worth it?" I asked softly.

Bres's expression immediately became shuttered. Any hint of vulnerability or emotion I thought I'd seen drifted away like the details of a dream upon waking. "You saw the files. You know what they did. What they do to innocent people who get in their way."

At his knowing look, I couldn't help but avert my gaze. Did he know I'd photographed the pages of the file he'd entrusted me with? I'd been stupid enough to uphold our deal and return the file to him after he helped me steal Dagda's cauldron from the Order, but not before I copied a number of the pages. Of course, he later screwed me over and stole the cauldron right back for them, so any guilt I felt was easily pushed aside.

For days after his betrayal, I'd combed the photographed copies for anything that would help me understand his actions better, but I was missing half the pages, and it was clear from his hard tone that I was also missing half the story. Instinct told me that his hatred of the Order was more than just a personal distaste for their code of ethics. He'd made significant sacrifices so that he'd be in a position to turn the tables on them when the time came. I just couldn't figure out what would be important enough for him to make revenge his sole purpose for living. Something told me I needed to read those pages again.

I sighed and shook my head. "I don't know where this all leaves us. Even if you were trying to protect me, I don't think I can trust you again."

"Good. You shouldn't."

CHAPTER THREE

"Where the hell were you?"

I looked up from the pages spread out in front of me as Teagan marched into the living room of her apartment, her black hair windswept and her expression harried.

"The Watchers," she said when I didn't immediately answer. "Brian. You were meant to meet us there. Remember?"

Grimacing, I glanced down at the time on my phone and belatedly noticed I had five missed calls and double that in unread messages. "Sorry. I just needed to clear my head after seeing Bres and…"

Teagan's expression softened marginally as I trailed off. Still, she wasn't quite ready to let me off the hook completely. "Brian was apoplectic when you didn't show. We need to be careful, Aisling. The last thing we need is the Watchers on our backs."

My shoulders slumped as I nodded. I knew she

was right, but I just hadn't had the emotional band-width for a head-to-head with Brian after my talk with Bres. The only thing I'd wanted to do when leaving his apartment was come home and reread the notes I'd copied from his file. It shouldn't matter to me what drove him, but I found it impossible to ignore the certainty that I was missing something important.

The printed pages spread around me had done little to shed light on my many questions. I had, however, found reference to a woman in some of the older notes that gave me pause.

Saoirse.

She was mentioned only once in the notes I had, so I'd previously overlooked it. But there was something different in the way he wrote about her, something softer, less detached. I had no idea if it was merely my imagination or my desperate attempt to find heart where there was none to find. I just knew I needed to look deeper.

"What happened with Bres?" Teagan asked, taking off her coat and coming to sit next to me on the sofa. She glanced with a raised eyebrow at the pages strewn haphazardly across the floor.

Tucking my feet up under me, I sighed. "He doesn't know where the cauldron is. They've moved all the artefacts from the HQ, and he doesn't know where they're being held now."

I didn't blame Teagan for the sceptical expression on her face, but to her credit, she remained quiet and waited for me to continue. A lump lodged itself in my throat.

"They hurt him. Bannon wanted him to bring me in, and he refused. So, they hurt him."

"Oh no, you don't." She pointed a warning finger at me. "Don't you dare start feeling sorry for him. This is what he wants, Ais – for you to feel bad so you'll overlook all the shitty things he's done to you."

I chewed my lip. She was most likely right, but it didn't stop the guilt from twisting my insides. I changed the subject.

"What are we going to do about the cauldron? He was our best bet for finding it."

"We forget about it." At my surprised look, Teagan held up a hand to halt my protest. "Even if we do find out where Bannon is keeping it, the chances of us getting it back are slim. I'll talk to Brian, see if the Watchers can do anything. Meanwhile, we need to focus our attention on finding the Claiming ritual."

I shuddered at the thought of the Watchers getting their hands on the cauldron and the magic it contained. But really, it would be no worse than the Order having it, so I let it go.

Standing, I gave my friend a tired smile. "I'll go talk nicely to the book for a while, see if it'll throw us a bone." I felt Teagan's concerned gaze follow me as I made my way to my bedroom.

The old leather book rested on my nightstand where I'd left it. I picked it up and settled back against the cushions on my bed, running my fingers tenderly over the cover. Faded with age, the lines in the leather were now as familiar to me as the lines on my own hand. Now that I understood the love and sacrifice that had gone into the tome, I felt an immense gratefulness to my ancestors. Having their words to guide me provided a comfort that I'd have never believed possible from ink on a page. I closed my eyes and sent up a silent prayer for them to provide that much-needed guidance now.

As I flicked open the book, my eyes immediately fell on the single reference to the Claiming that I'd come across to date. My ancestor's opening letter made it clear that the Tuatha were willing to sacrifice every-thing to prevent the Fomorians from completing the ritual. That alone was enough to convince me the Order couldn't be allowed to, either. I only hoped that less sacrifice was required this time.

I turned the pages, curious to see what the book would present to me today. Some of the entries seemed to be permanent fixtures – presumably because the information they contained was vital knowledge. Others changed as if sensing exactly what I needed in the moment. I came to one such page now and stopped.

Rare lunar events.

Curious, I scanned the top paragraph. It gave a brief overview of the lunar cycle and how it affected the presence of magic in our world. Some of the terms I was familiar with, while others were new to me. It was the last paragraph that gave me pause.

Some such events are so rare that most of us will not witness them within our lifetime. Some of these events can result in a shift so great that most of us hope we do not.

Well, that wasn't ominous at all.

Was this part of the Claiming ritual? Did the Order need some rare cosmic set of events to enact their plan? If that was the case, then we'd only need to make sure they missed their window of opportunity.

A tentative hope surged within me.

Stopping the Order once was a much more preferable option than having the threat of the Claiming hanging over us forever and a day. Maybe if we could figure out what rare lunar events were due to happen soon, it would give us a starting point to pre-empt their plans.

I turned my attention back to the book, but blinked as my vision grew hazy at the edges. The room faded around me, and when I blinked again, I found myself standing at the centre of a green field covered in mist. Seven large standing stones surrounded me.

Hissing in a breath, I turned in a slow circle, every muscle in my body tense. I hadn't been back to the Church of the Blessed Heart or the ritual site since the face-off with Dub and Carmen, but it was unmistakably where I found myself now.

As I completed my wary circle, a person emerged from the mist, making their way towards me.

Instinctively, I reached for my magic. It came quicker than it had even before the cauldron drained me. I held it at the ready, comforted by its presence and the fact I wasn't wholly defenceless this time.

The person's features grew clearer as the distance between us lessened. She was tall with an almost regal bearing, and long strawberry-blonde hair flowed out behind her silk dress. The same green silk as the sash I'd kept the book cocooned in for months.

Recognition filled me, bringing with it a sense of dread.

I'd seen this woman before, in the visions that had haunted my waking and sleeping hours, back when this whole mess had begun. And in the tapestry that had hung on the museum wall at the Order's HQ. I'd never learned her name or what role she played in the sacrifice the Tuatha made. But she had tried to warn me then, and I had a bad feeling her presence here didn't bode well now.

She came to a stop about ten feet from me, her pale skin practically glowing in the eerie mist that surrounded us. There was a sadness in her eyes as they met mine, and I pulled my magic tighter around me.

"Time is running out."

I flinched as the woman's voice surrounded me like an echo fading on the air.

"You need to find him before it's too late. A decision must be made. A price must be paid. Find him."

And with that, my vision faded.

CHAPTER FOUR

The bedroom reappeared around me, but the sense of foreboding stayed. I hadn't had a vision since I completed the ritual to release magic, and though I could see no reason why that might change now, I was fairly certain I hadn't fallen asleep.

A glance down confirmed that the book still lay open on my lap at the last page I remembered reading. The light in the room had faded considerably while I'd been ... elsewhere, and I felt night's oppressive weight pressing down on me like sand running through a timer. The woman had ordered me to "find him," and I could think of only one person she might be referring to.

Killian had been absent for over a week now from my dreams – ever since he'd trapped Dub and Carmen's consciousness in the dreamscape to protect me. On the rare occasions when the dreamscape did appear, I'd been alone in the meadow with only my thoughts for company. With each passing night, my concern for him had grown until it became almost suffocating.

Was he hurt?

Had Dub and Carmen somehow managed to trap *him*?

Was this all because he'd tried to help me?

After a few days, the concern had turned into anger. It was stupid, really, but it was the safer emotion. I couldn't bear thinking that something had happened to Killian because of me, and I didn't know what to do about his absence. So, I clung to the anger, fully intending to give him a piece of my mind when he did reappear.

With the woman's warning echoing in my ears, I knew I could no longer allow myself the luxury of clinging to that hope. Killian needed me, and I was damn well going to find him.

Carefully, I closed the book and put it back on my nightstand. I didn't bother undressing for bed; my aim for tonight wasn't a restful sleep. With my thoughts focused one hundred percent on the dreamscape, I drifted off.

Darkness was the first thing to greet me. I fought against it, refusing to be swayed from my mission as my subconscious worked to will the dreamscape to life. It took long enough that I worried it wouldn't work. Then finally, my surroundings changed. A familiar meadow appeared around me. Soft grass cushioned me where I sat. But for the first time since I began coming here, I couldn't feel the warmth of the sun on my skin. Frowning, I looked up.

With a hissed breath, I took in the sky above me. It was the same clear blue as always, only this time there was one key difference. A dark, jagged crack ran across its length.

Goosebumps prickled my arms as I took in the void just barely visible on the other side of the crack. The last few times I'd been to the dreamscape, something had felt off – aside from Killian's absence, that was. I hadn't been able to put my finger on exactly what was wrong, but it was clear my concerns hadn't been unfounded. What the hell could cause cracks in the sky?

Driven by a newfound sense of urgency, I stood and scanned my surroundings. Aside from the occasional magic lesson that had us exploring the woods bordering the meadow, I hadn't had much cause to explore the dreamscape. I'd been naturally curious about the world that was as real to me as my waking one, but there had been so much to learn and far too many instances of my life being in mortal peril. When your time was limited, you had to prioritise.

Because of that, I now had only my instincts to guide me on which direction to go. I focused my attention on that place at the centre of my core where my magic resided. Turning left and right, I waited for a sign, for some sense that would point me in the right direction. When it didn't come, I sighed in resignation and just started walking straight ahead.

As I made my way into the trees, shadows enveloped me. There were none of the sounds you would normally expect. In fact, the trees all seemed eerily silent. I had the strangest thought that maybe it was all really a movie set, and a nervous giggle bubbled up inside me. Half afraid I would come to a cliff that fell away to nothing, I ploughed on.

After a few minutes, daylight once more broke through the trees. I hurried towards it, and relief loosened some of the tension in my body as I stepped out from beneath the shadowy canopy of leaves. A vast valley opened up before me, rolling green hills surrounding it.

My first thought was how beautiful the view was, but as I took in the scene in more detail, I had the same sense that something wasn't right. Rather than deterring me, it just spurred me on, because at the centre of the valley, I could see what looked like a small, grey house. I quickly located a trail that looked well-trodden and began my descent.

By the time I reached the bottom, I was all but running for the old stone house that reminded me of many of the ruins dotted around the Irish countryside. Was this it? Was this where Killian lived?

"Killian?" I called loudly, not once considering the possibility that I should proceed with caution. "Killian? Are you here?"

When my magical dream tutor didn't immediately pop out and say "surprise" in his usual droll tone, my steps slowed. Doubt crept in, and with it, the familiar fear that something terrible had happened to Killian because of me.

I came to a stop in front of the wooden door that had clearly been fashioned from one of the trees surrounding the valley. My hand shook as I reached out and rapped on its hard surface. The sound reverberated back at me only to be followed by silence, but the door moved slightly. Hesitantly, I pushed it open.

The space beyond was dark except for the streaks of daylight that seeped in through the doorway. It took my eyes a moment to adjust to the gloom and make out a small square space, probably no more than ten feet by ten feet. At the wall furthest from the door, a bed had been fashioned atop a low wooden frame covered in thick woollen blankets. A figure lay curled up on the bed with their back to me.

Relief filled me as I recognised Killian's dark, jaw-length hair and lean frame. The feeling quickly turned to panic as I realised he hadn't reacted to my presence in the slightest and didn't seem to be moving.

I rushed to his side. Fear slithered through me and left me cold as I crouched down next to him. "Killian." I shook him. "Killian, wake up."

He groaned in response, and my knees went weak.

Killian rolled onto his back and blinked groggily up at me. "Aisling?"

Confusion tinged his tone, and he seemed to be struggling to keep his eyes open as he looked up at me. Even in the gloom of the space, I could make out the dark circles beneath his eyes, and the heavy stubble that covered his jaw. He looked exhausted.

"Where have you been? What the hell is going on? I've been so worried." Oops, hadn't meant for that to come out so harshly.

He scrubbed a hand over his face and tried to rise to sitting. His arm buckled beneath him, but he caught himself – just about.

I slipped my arm behind his back and helped him up. The fact he didn't protest the help worried me more than his obvious exhaustion. I crouched down in front of him and searched his face.

"Killian, what's going on?" I asked, more gently this time. "You haven't shown in over a week, and now there's this huge crack in the sky..."

He looked away, not meeting my eyes. "I'm sorry. It's complicated."

"Is this because you helped me with Dub and Carmen?" My voice cracked as I asked the question, the fear that I'd been trying to suppress all these nights now forcing its way to the surface at my newfound certainty that something wasn't right.

Understanding sparked some life in his dark eyes and he shook his head, reaching up to cup my cheek. "No. This is not your fault. None of this is your fault."

I leaned into the warmth of his hand, the relief at feeling his touch, solid and real, almost overwhelming, but still not enough to chase away my bone-deep chill. "But you brought them here, and now everything feels wrong. And you won't tell me what's going on."

Gently, he tilted my chin up. "I had to keep you safe. And I would do it again. What's happening here was always meant to happen. It's just accelerating now."

I frowned, trying to make sense of his words. "What do you mean?"

"The dreamscape was only ever meant to be temporary. It was where the magic was held in stasis until you released it. I guess you could call it a battery of sorts. As the magic returns to your world, the battery runs down until eventually it's empty."

I hissed in a breath, drawing back from him as if placing distance between us would make what he was saying less true. Because I couldn't – no, wouldn't – allow myself to think what that might mean for Killian.

"This place hasn't changed in all the time I've been coming here. Why now? Why is it accelerating?"

Killian gave a self-deprecating laugh and ran a hand through his hair. "When I brought Dub and Carmen here, I didn't account for their magic. It was a stupid oversight on my part, really. Their magic doesn't like being contained. It has been trying to return alongside the rest of the magic. That's why I haven't been around. All of my energy has been focused on trying to hold it back, and it's weakening me. It's weakening the structure of this place."

My chest constricted with the instinctual panic on remembering their vile dark magic. "What happens if the magic does return?"

I didn't think it was possible for Killian's expression to get any grimmer. Turned out I was wrong.

"I don't know," he admitted. "So long as Dub and Carmen's consciousnesses are held here, the magic is unbound. There's a risk it might merge with the earth's magic and corrupt it. Or it may be free for somebody to Claim it."

There was that damn capital C again. Worry settled over me as I considered exactly who might be interested in doing just that.

"Killian. What happens to you once the battery runs down?"

CHAPTER FIVE

I clung on for all I was worth, but the dreamscape faded and the last remnants of sleep left me. *No.* I needed to go back. He hadn't answered my question. Panic stole the breath from my chest as my eyes snapped open. Killian. I had to go back. What if next time I fell asleep, the dreamscape wasn't there? What if he wasn't?

Jolting upright, I allowed defiance to push back against the panic that threatened to swamp me. I refused to accept that as a possibility. Yes, I had seen the changes for myself and had no choice but to take Killian's word on what was happening. But I refused to believe that after multiple lifetimes of sacrifice, his fate was to just fade away with the dreamscape. I wouldn't allow it.

Determination burned in my veins as I flung the covers off. I knew from the light streaming in around the edges of my curtains that I wouldn't be going back to sleep, so I'd do the next best thing – research. Killian needed my help. He was draining himself dry to make sure Dub and Carmen's dark magic stayed contained. The least I could do was find a way to help him. Maybe if we could sort that problem, it would buy us more time to deal with the issue of what happened to him once the dreamscape went kablooey.

Teagan was already sitting at the kitchen island when I came into the room. She glanced up from the newspaper she was reading. "Oh good, you're up. We need to get moving soon if…"

Her forehead creased in a frown as she trailed off, no doubt taking in what I could only assume was the slightly manic expression on my face. "What's wrong?" she demanded.

The words lodged in my throat, and the panic that still lurked at the edges of my awareness threatened to surge once more. I swallowed hard and pulled out one of the high stools to sit next to her. Taking a moment to compose my thoughts, I finally said, "Killian's in trouble."

It took only a couple of minutes to bring her up to speed, given my own understanding of the situation was depressingly lacking. She stayed quiet as I filled her in, but I didn't miss the way her eyes darkened in concern.

An idle part of my brain wondered if her banshee abilities would allow her to sense if Killian's life was in danger. Technically, he was thousands of years old. Was he even alive in the same sense we were? I had no idea. I just knew he was alive to me, and I needed to make sure he stayed that way.

"What do we do?" I dropped my head in my hands, the back of my throat burning.

Teagan reached over and rubbed my back, her hand moving in comforting circles. "We'll figure it out. I promise. We'll get started on research as soon as we're back from the Watchers."

The Watchers? Oh shit, the meeting that had been rescheduled from the day before.

I jerked my head up, about to protest about priorities, but Teagan held up a hand to stop me. "I know it's the last thing you want to do, but you didn't see Brian when you failed to show up. I'm not joking, Aisling. I really think he'll follow through with his threat to throw you in prison if you don't do some serious ass-kissing today."

Even if Brian couldn't explain enough about the two unconscious bodies – or his role in moving them – to make charges stick, I couldn't afford to lose time by being hauled down to a police station for questioning. So, whether I liked it or not, Teagan was right.

I clenched my fists and bit back a scream of frustration as I stood. "Fine. Let's get it over with."

Getting ready in record time, I was waiting by the door for Teagan when Pete sent a message to say he was parked outside the gates, waiting for us. We locked up and made our way down in the lift. The weather was grey and dreary, and I pulled my coat tighter around me as I stepped outside. It matched my mood perfectly, and I tried not to take it as a bad omen.

I was about to suggest to Teagan that we pack it all in and move to a sunny desert island when a man walked through the gates towards us. My footsteps stalled, and my lungs forgot to complete the expansion they were midway through. The man's stoic expression didn't so much as crack at my reaction – he just continued his clipped pace until he came to a stop three feet from us. I took in the navy pinstripe suit and the black eye patch, and instinctively drew my magic to me.

Bill, the "museum curator" for the Order of the Fomori, inclined his head. "Ms. O'Meara, what a pleasure to see you again."

"I think we can safely say the pleasure is all yours." Teagan stepped closer to my side. Her whole body was tensed, and I had no doubt she was ready to interject if he so much as twitched a muscle in a way she didn't like.

Bill didn't acknowledge her. Given he was well aware of her banshee nature, the fact he didn't seem even slightly disconcerted by her presence was worrying. What kind of person wasn't afraid of someone who could make your brains leak out of your skull?

"I have been asked to deliver this to you." Bill held out a small white envelope with my name embossed in flowing silver script on its surface. "The Order are holding a charity fundraiser this evening, and Mr. Bannon requests the pleasure of your company."

I almost choked. "A charity fundraiser? Are you serious?"

"Indeed. It is important that we are seen to be active with our political agenda. The event also affords you and Mr. Bannon a chance to speak on neutral territory."

"Why the hell would I want to speak with him?"

"There is much that needs to be discussed regarding ... upcoming events."

My blood went cold. He was talking about the Claiming. He had to be.

Unwilling to even hint that I knew what he was referring to, I demanded, "Where's the cauldron?"

Bill looked down his nose at me. "That is of no concern to you."

Magic flared through my veins in response to my anger, and I clenched my fists to quell the urge to punch him. "It is if said cauldron contains my magic and is in the hands of a less-than-reputable person."

"Indeed. One would think that a 'less-than-reputable person' might be inclined to use that magic to encourage your compliance. It's a good thing Mr. Bannon is not such a person."

Except he was, and we all knew it.

The unspoken threat hung in the air between us, represented by the innocuous white envelope Bill still held out to me. What would he do if I refused to take it?

Before I could decide on my next move, footsteps sounded at the gate.

"What's taking you two so..." Pete trailed off as he rounded the corner and took in the sight of me and Teagan facing off with Bill. Tension coiled through his body, and his eyes flashed amber for a moment before they returned to their usual brown and settled coldly on the museum curator.

"Bill here was just inviting Aisling to meet his psycho boss at some bullshit political event they're putting on to convince the public they care about the little folk," Teagan informed him, her gaze never once straying from the Order member before us.

"Is that so?"

I shivered at the hint of a growl that edged Pete's tone and decided we needed to get this wrapped up ASAP before things started getting messy. Grabbing Teagan's hand, I tugged her in Pete's direction. "Tell Bannon we have nothing to discuss."

Bill's features tightened, though his expression didn't change. "I'll be sure to pass along the message. Make no mistake, however. A conversation *will* be had. It is up to you whether that conversation is amicable or not."

CHAPTER SIX

I was still shaking by the time Pete pulled the car to a stop outside the Watchers HQ. I'd only released the hold on my magic once we were on the motorway and there were many miles between us and Teagan's apartment. I kept it close to the surface though, unable to let go of the illogical fear that someone from the Order would magically appear in the car next to me at any moment.

As we climbed out of the car in front of the large industrial-style building, I was even more pissed off that I was being forced to waste time here. Killian's life could very well be hanging in the balance, and Bill's appearance was a clear warning that I was back on the Order's radar. I couldn't help feeling that time was against me, and the last thing I needed was to waste it arguing with the Watchers.

Clearly sensing my edginess, Teagan gave me a

warning look. "Play nice, and we'll get out of here quicker."

I didn't bother acknowledging the comment.

Pete pulled open one of the large glass doors and stepped aside so that we could pass.

The sour-faced receptionist looked up as we entered, her expression anything but friendly. "Take a seat. Brian will see you shortly."

Pete and Teagan looked at each other with raised eyebrows, and I struggled to hold back my smirk. I was used to being a less-than-welcome sight here at the Watchers' headquarters. They, however, had both been star students up until recently and had no doubt enjoyed more freedom than was ever extended to me. With recent events changing the status quo, they apparently were going to have to slum it with me.

We settled ourselves on one of the cream sofas that lined the edges of the reception area. A large clock hung on the wall behind the desk and the seconds ticked to minutes, each one that passed nicely punctuating the point that we were not the ones in charge here. Almost thirty minutes had gone by before Brian finally appeared, by which point I'd been ready to walk out ten times over. Only Teagan's firm grip on my arm had stopped me.

Brian's expression was unreadable as he strode towards us, and I couldn't tell if the tension in his shoulders was from lifting too many weights or a warning for what was to come.

"Follow me." Without another word, he turned on

his heel and headed for a door, almost hidden in the wood panelling that formed the backdrop of the reception.

"Sorry for being late," I muttered. "Nice to see you."

Teagan elbowed me in the side to shush my quiet rant, but I could tell by the tight line of her mouth that she was less than impressed by the greeting too. It also didn't escape my attention when she and Pete flanked me on either side, acting almost like bodyguards. Whether they were aiming to keep me safe from the Watchers or the Watchers safe from me, I wasn't sure.

The corridor Brian led us down was different from any I'd been through on previous occasions. We passed only a couple of doors along the entire space, and none had a sign outside to indicate what lay beyond. Finally, we reached what looked like a fire exit at the end of the corridor.

Brian pushed the bar down and opened the door to reveal a nondescript square room. A large oval table occupied the space, and one wall of the room was covered by a large screen. Three of the eight chairs surrounding the table were occupied, and I took in the woman and two men with a growing sense of unease.

A red-headed man, seated in the chair furthest from the door, glared at me with barely concealed animosity. Richie. The name was a vague memory from my one and only past encounter with him. I'd stumbled upon him and some other Watchers in the training centre when I'd last accompanied Teagan here in her brief stint as a lab rat. He'd made it clear then that he was far from my biggest fan, and that obviously hadn't changed.

The woman to his left had salt-and-pepper hair tied back in a severe pony tail at the base of her neck. I recognised her as the Watcher who had intervened when Richie was mouthing off, but I hadn't caught her name, and her hard expression didn't exactly give me the warm and fuzzies. The final man next to her was thin and wiry with black hair cut tight to his head. He didn't even spare us a glance as we stepped into the room, his attention glued to the laptop in front of him.

Brian closed the door and motioned for us to take the three seats across from the Watchers. In the most blatant power play of the morning so far, he remained standing at the head of the table.

"Now that we're all finally here" – he shot a pointed glare in my direction – "we'll get straight down to business."

I held up my hand to halt his little speech before he could continue. "Maybe we can start by clarifying who 'all' is? We weren't aware that other Watchers were joining the meeting this morning."

Brian's expression turned from somewhat stony to granite, and I could have sworn he was mentally counting to ten before he responded. "Richie, Kate, and Eamonn have been appointed to work with you on the PR team."

"The PR team…"

"Yes. You know the one you now work for as PR representative for the Watchers."

I swallowed the urge to tell him where he could shove his job and pasted a sweet smile on my face. "I don't believe I've received my contract yet."

Richie leaned back in his chair and narrowed his eyes, animosity rolling off him like a physical force. "Probably because you were busy swanning off on holidays while the grownups were cleaning up your mess – again."

My mouth dropped open and I stared at him. Was he for real? A homicidal maniac and his equally psychopathic mother tried to kill me, and I was being berated for needing a few days away to clear my head?

"You seem to have your facts wrong," I told him with a calm I most certainly did not feel. "We" – I indicated to myself, Teagan, and Pete – "cleaned up the mess and handed it to you in a nice little unconscious package. The Watchers didn't even have to break a sweat."

"That doesn't make you tough," Kate said, looking me square in the eye. "That makes you stupid. You risked your life, and your friends' lives, all because you didn't want to be a team player and ask for help."

"I've seen the conditions that your help comes with," I retorted, magic flaring at my core as my anger grew. Teagan reached over and squeezed my knee, but I was in no place to heed her warning.

Kate placed a hand on the table, and frost began to spread from beneath her fingers.

"Enough!" Brian demanded.

I blinked and the frost was gone. Kate drew her

hand back and folded her arms across her chest, no longer looking at me.

"Aisling, you will be working with Richie, Kate, and Eamonn for the foreseeable future, so I suggest the four of you make an effort to get along."

Any protest I might make died on my tongue at the cold look he turned my way. I swallowed hard, silently reminding myself that I wouldn't be able to help Killian if Brian decided to make life hard for me.

"Can I at least ask what it is I'm meant to be doing in this new role?"

"Whatever we need you to do. Your first assignment is tonight. You and your team will attend a charity event being run by the Order of the Fomori. It is a political event, so it's expected that the media will be present."

My blood ran cold. The Order's charity event? Surely he couldn't be serious.

Next to me, Teagan had also tensed. "What possible reason could you have for putting her directly in the Order's sights?"

Brian looked unconcerned by the potential risk to my safety. "We have reason to believe they will offload an ancient artefact at the auction. We need to know who it goes to."

"That makes no sense," I objected. "Why would the Order willingly hand away power?"

"Precisely what we want to know. And what you're going to find out for us."

CHAPTER SEVEN

I tugged self-consciously at the thin straps holding my dress up. The sheer black fabric clung to each of my curves before falling effortlessly to skim the ground. The outfit was about as impractical as it got for walking into a den of vipers. So, of course Brian had insisted I wear it.

"Stop fidgeting," Teagan ordered as she put what had to be the hundredth pin into my mass of blonde curls. "You look gorgeous."

"Bannon is going to think I'm there because of his invitation," I griped, not for the first time. "Or should I say, his threat."

"Brian said you had to attend. He didn't say you had to make your presence known. Besides, it's a masquerade gala. If you're lucky, nobody will recognise you."

I took a slow breath and tried to let go of the tension that had been tying me up in knots all afternoon. She was right. I'd keep a low profile – or as low as I could with three babysitters in tow – get the information Brian wanted, and get the hell out.

Turning to my friend, I grabbed her hands, beseeching. "And you promise you'll get started on the research?"

"Stop worrying. I have it under control. Pete will be here to help as soon as he's checked in on your mam. Just promise me you'll be careful."

I nodded and attempted a reassuring smile. The damage to the dreamscape had been playing on my mind all day, but I hadn't had a moment to even consider where we might start looking for answers. If anyone could find them, it was Teagan. But the last thing I wanted to do was waste time at the damn charity event when I could be helping her instead.

The buzz of my phone sent my nerves shooting through the roof once more. "Guess that's my summons."

My palms were suddenly clammy and butterflies danced around my insides. I gave one final check that I had everything in my bag. Then, with nothing left to stall for, I grabbed my mask.

A black Mercedes idled outside the gates to the apartment complex. I slowed my steps as I approached, squinting to make sure it actually was the Watchers waiting for me and not the Order being presumptuous asses.

The passenger window lowered to reveal Richie's sneering face. "What do you want, a red-carpet invitation? Get in." He jerked his head towards the rear door, then turned his attention forward. And just like that, I was dismissed.

This is going to be a fun car ride.

Muttering under my breath, I opened the door and slid into the back seat next to Eamonn. His face was illuminated by the screen of a handheld computer, and he barely even seemed aware of my presence. Kate sat in the driver's seat wearing a green silk dress that looked like it was more suited to lounging in the back of a chauffeur-driven limousine. She gave me the barest nod of acknowledgement, and we were off.

The drive to the Shelbourne Hotel was far too short for my liking. As we pulled up at the front where valets waited to relieve us of our car, I scanned the faces of the security guards stationed outside the hotel. I didn't recognise any of them as the men who'd held guns on us at the Church of the Blessed Heart, but I had no doubt they were all Order goons.

The three Watchers climbed out of the car to join the gathering crowd of men and women who milled about, talking to reporters and posing for photographs. Heart beating a tad faster than normal, I pulled my mask down over my eyes and prayed like hell it would be enough to stop anyone from recognising me as I followed them.

"Ms. O'Meara?"

I jerked my head up and my pulse leapt into my throat as I found myself face-to-face with the broad chest of a black-clad security guard.

"I was asked to escort you to the VIP section when you arrived."

My mouth went dry as I took in his bulky frame and unyielding expression. The three Watchers who were meant to be babysitting me had been neatly shunted to the side, and if the stormy look on Kate's face was anything to go by, this wasn't part of their plan for the evening. Which could only mean the instruction had come from Bannon.

"Oh, I prefer to slum it with the common folk." My laugh came out strained, and I cringed inwardly.

The security guard didn't budge an inch as I attempted to step around him to rejoin my companions. Curious gazes began to turn in our direction, and my cheeks heated.

When the guard swept his arm out for me to proceed, I had no choice but to comply or risk making a scene. Reluctantly, I made my way along the red carpet towards the hotel entrance. The Watchers moved to follow, but the guard held up a hand to stop them.

"Your team will be shown to the press area," he informed me as two further guards stepped up to lead the trio away.

I swallowed my protest, knowing it would be fruitless. This was a public event. Surely Bannon wouldn't be stupid enough to pull anything too crazy here.

Clinging to that thought, I gave one final glance back to see Kate, Richie, and Eamonn being led away to what I hoped was the press area. Then I followed the guard into the hotel.

As we walked, I searched for any opportunity to escape my escort. We had just reached the lobby and were heading towards large double doors that led to a ballroom when I spotted a queue of women. The toilets!

"Um, I need to use the ladies' room," I said in a hurry.

Not waiting for the security guard to protest or stop me, I hurried to join the back of the queue. I "accidentally" stumbled as did, bumping into the brunette in front of me.

"Oh, I'm so sorry," I gushed with an apologetic smile. "These shoes are lethal. They have my balance all over the place."

She waved away my apology with a knowing laugh. "Oh, trust me. I get it," she said, hoisting her dress to show off her own sky-high stilettos.

From the corner of my eye, I could see my escort looming. He was twitching with the urge to come and haul me from the line, and only the need not to cause a scene was stopping him. So, I kept up the small talk as the queue inched forward. I wasn't quite sure what I planned to do once I reached the toilets, but as I finally stepped through the door to find myself in a window-less room, my heart sank. No impromptu escapes out the window for me. Maybe if I took the longest pee in history, the guard would get bored waiting for me and leave?

Since I knew that was unlikely to happen, I decided not to torture the line of women behind me by holding up one of the stalls. Instead, I took my time fixing my makeup in the mirror and tried to figure out a way to get myself out of this damn situation.

"I love your mask. It's absolutely stunning!"

I turned in surprise to the redhead next to me and smiled. "Thanks. Yours is gorgeous too."

She made a face in the mirror. "I hate it. My boyfriend bought it for me as a present. It doesn't really go with my dress, but I didn't want to hurt his feelings. You know how it is."

I took in the sleek blue dress she wore and the intricate gold mask. The combination didn't look bad, but it wasn't what I'd have picked either. An idea formed in my mind, and I latched onto it.

"I know exactly what you mean." I nodded conspiratorially. "I'm not too attached to my one, to be honest. If you wanted to swap, I'd be more than happy to."

Her eyes lit up with interest. "You'd do that?"

I began to undo my mask before doubt could kick in. "Sure. I'm here for work anyway, so I'm really not too bothered. And everything goes with black. Your boyfriend will be none the wiser."

That last point seemed to do the trick, and she eagerly undid her mask to swap with me. The gold mask didn't magically transform me into a whole new person, but I hoped it would be enough to confuse the situation.

I spotted another woman in a black dress about to

leave, so I bid the redhead farewell and hurried to exit alongside the other woman. As I did, I pulled some magic to me from my surroundings and let it pool in my core.

With practice, I'd become reasonably adept at low-level elemental magic. I figured a little extra distraction might help me now, so I focused my attention on the air and sent a burst of wind towards the reception desk. Papers flew up in the air, and there were some shouts of surprise as a mask or two went flying. Oops, might have overestimated my force on that one.

Not waiting to see if I'd been spotted, I hurried for the ballroom and the crowd I could see gathering there.

Waitstaff in crisp black attire milled about with trays of champagne, and the offering of free bubbly had encouraged people to congregate at the rear of the ballroom. Beyond them, rows of seats had been laid out across the width of the room. A roped-off section separated what I assumed to be the VIP area in a way that was subtle enough not to seem exclusionary, and at the topmost end of the room, a stage had been erected. A wooden podium was carefully placed off to one side so as not to obscure the black cloth backdrop, upon which the Order's political agenda was being projected. And standing next to the podium, talking quietly to the security guard who had been escorting me, was Declan Bannon.

Bannon turned and scanned the room once before nodding.

Though I knew it was unlikely he'd be able to spot me among the crowd from this distance, I stepped back, feeling like a hunted animal caught in the crosshairs.

Screw this. I didn't care what Brian wanted. I wasn't staying here any longer. I pivoted on my heel, more than ready to leave. And smacked straight into a solid chest, clad in a pristine black suit.

"I've been looking for you."

CHAPTER EIGHT

"What the hell are you doing here?" I ground out, my fists clenched as my heart tried to hammer its way out of my chest. "I thought you and the Order weren't buddies anymore."

Bres's grin was smug, and his blue eyes sparkled with mischief behind the simple turquoise mask that covered the top half of his face. The urge to punch him was almost overwhelming.

"We're not. I just figured you might need someone to save you – again. Besides..." His gaze heated as he ran his eyes down the length of my body. "It gives me a chance to see you wearing that."

Heat pooled at my core and I glared, clinging to anger as the safer emotion. "And how exactly do you plan on saving me?"

"Like this."

Before his words could even register, he grabbed

my hand and swung me around, pushing me back into a shadowy recess behind us. His body pressed flush against mine and heat seared my skin through the thin material of my dress. His right arm pressed against the wall above my head, and he trailed the fingers of his other hand across my cheek.

A shiver ran through me as he leaned his head down. His breath ran along my neck like a gentle caress.

"You look stunning," he whispered in my ear.

He stepped back just as suddenly, leaving me cold and blinking dumbly at the space between us. Embarrassment heated my cheeks as common sense rushed back in and slapped me upside the head. What the hell was I doing?

Bres shifted his body slightly, and I caught sight of the security guards weaving their way through the crowd of people. They were clearly looking for someone, and if I had to guess, I'd say it was me. Understanding dawned as I noted how Bres's body was effectively shielding me from sight.

For some illogical reason, disappointment settled like lead in my gut. It was quickly replaced by anger – this time at myself for being so stupid.

"What are you doing here?" I demanded again, smoothing down the front of my dress just so I could do something with my trembling hands. I thought I saw something like regret flash in his eyes, but it was gone so quickly I wasn't sure if it was my imagination.

"The Order aren't holding this auction for the good of the people. They're up to something, and I need to know what it is."

Yep, there was that disappointment again. God, I was so stupid. Had I really thought he'd been serious when he'd said he was here for me?

Before I could even attempt to make sense of how that made me feel, a man with grey hair and small glasses perched on his nose stepped up behind the podium and tapped the microphone. "Ladies and gentlemen, if I could please invite you all to take your seats. The auction is about to begin."

The crowd began to disperse towards the seating area and I pressed back further into the shadows. Should I find a random seat near the back and hope nobody spotted me? Should I seek out the Watchers? I could just about make out the press area on the far side of the ballroom, but couldn't see any sight of Kate or the two men amongst the camera crews and reporters.

Bres moved to my side, placing a hand on the small of my back. "Stay here with me. Bannon will have people watching the seats for you."

"And how do I know you're not going to deliver me to Bannon yourself? It would be one way to get back in his good books."

"I've never been in Bannon's good books. Why would that change now?"

I didn't know exactly what to say to that, so I said nothing as everyone finished taking their seats. A hush fell over the room. The auctioneer spread his arms wide, and the drape backdrop behind him parted to reveal the lots to be auctioned. A thrum of magic instantly washed over me.

"Welcome, ladies and gentlemen. It is our great honour to have you here today to contribute towards a more positive Ireland. All donations made during the auction will go towards creating a better future for the homeless of our nation. Not only that, but whatever amount is raised here tonight will be matched in full by the Order themselves."

Rapturous applause erupted from the crowd. I gritted my teeth, but somehow managed to restrain myself from commenting on the Order's sudden philanthropic nature. Instead, I focused my attention on the items lined up in display cases along the back of the stage. The lights above them remained dim so I couldn't see any of the lots clearly, but I was certain Brian had been right – there was something powerful among them.

The first few lots passed by uneventfully. A beautiful painting fetched a not insubstantial twenty thousand euro, while an antique broach resulted in a bidding war that ended at almost fifty thousand. As impressive as the values were, none of the objects struck me as the cause of the magical current raising the hairs on my arms.

"Do you know what it is?" I asked Bres. I hadn't missed the tension that radiated from him, or the way he watched every lot being brought forward like a hawk.

"If I had to guess, I'd say it's something relevant to the Claiming. The Order don't do anything without a purpose. If they're auctioning off something of power, it's because it suits their endgame, not out of the goodness of their heart."

I snorted. It didn't take a genius to figure that much out. Though Bres's theory of it being something related to the Claiming disquieted me.

"You're still expecting the Claiming to go ahead then?" I tried to keep the question casual, but I was pretty sure I failed. I'd been clear about my refusal to help him, hadn't I?

"The Claiming will go ahead. The Order will make sure of it. The only question is who does the Claiming."

He gave me a pointed look, which I did my best to ignore. This wasn't the time and place for debate, and I sure as hell wasn't interested in debating my decision.

Still, I couldn't help but ask, "Why is this so important to you, Bres? I get that the Order are evil, and I completely agree with not wanting them to have more power. But there's more to it than what you're telling me."

His eyes darkened and a muscle twitched at the side of his jaw. For the longest time, I didn't think he'd answer. When he finally spoke, his words were so low that I wasn't sure if I'd imagined them.

"I need to do it for her. So that she can be proud of me."

"Our final lot of the evening is the most special of all," the auctioneer announced, dragging my attention back to the stage even as an inexplicable surge of jealousy rose within me.

The auctioneer's assistant stepped forward with a long wooden box in his arms and instantly I knew this was the source of the magic I'd been sensing. Apprehension clenched my insides. Without thinking, I reached out and gripped Bres's arm to steady myself. His whole body was tense beneath my touch.

"Believed to date back before the time of Christ, this stunning work of craftsmanship is any collector's dream," the auctioneer continued.

As he spoke, the assistant raised the lid on the wooden box and an audible gasp rippled through the room. I leaned forward, a familiar draw urging me to close the distance between myself and the artefact I'd last seen hanging on the wall in Bannon's secret room.

The gleaming sword lay nestled upon a bed of green silk. It seemed almost simple in comparison to the lots that had come before it. But there was no mistaking the power that emanated from the artefact, and if the rapt expressions of the audience members was anything to go by, I wasn't the only one who noticed it.

The auctioneer continued to wax lyrical about the possible origins of the artefact, but his words faded to little more than a drone in my ears. Every part of my being was focused on one thing – the sword.

A sharp pain in my arm snapped the room back into focus, breaking through the haze my thoughts had become. I looked in surprise at Bres, who was gripping my upper arm tightly, something like concern darkening his eyes.

"Sorry, but you looked like you were about to bolt up onto the stage and take the sword from the guy's hands."

I looked down. Sure enough, I'd taken a few steps forward and my body was straining against his hold. What the hell? Shivering, I huddled back into the shadows and wrapped my arms around myself.

"We start the bidding at €100,000," the auctioneer declared.

To my shock, more than one hand shot up in the air. A buzz of excitement filled the room and in a matter of minutes, the bidding had reached almost half a million. Who were these people that they had that kind of money to throw away? And what hope was there of keeping the Order out of power if they had people like this behind them?

The thought chilled me to the core, and a sense of hopelessness pressed down upon me.

Movement from the crowd drew my gaze as a woman in an A-line black dress stood. Unlike most of the other men and women in attendance, she wore no mask and her attire was more suited to a boardroom.

Her expression gave nothing away as she held up her paddle.

"Five million."

Mine wasn't the only shocked gasp as all eyes in the room turned to look at her. Next to me, Bres sucked in a breath.

The gravel dropped with a resounding thump.

I looked at Bres, frowning. "What the hell just happened?"

A grim expression was my only response.

CHAPTER NINE

Within minutes of the final lot being sold, the room became a buzz of excited conversation, with everyone rising from their seats to mingle. I scanned the crowd to try and catch sight of the woman in the black dress, but she was nowhere to be seen.

I chewed my lip, debating what to do. There was no doubt in my mind that the sword was the artefact Brian had sent me here to monitor. Somehow I doubted he'd be satisfied with "a random woman bought it for five million, then disappeared" as my report for the evening. Maybe I should try to find the Watchers? They might have seen where the woman went.

I turned, intending to quiz Bres about anything he might know, but stopped as I spotted the auctioneer striding towards me. In complete contrast to the three large, scowling security guards at his back, the man had a wide smile on his face as he held a long wooden box before him.

My pulse ratcheted up, and every muscle in my body tensed. Adrenaline flooded my system, demanding that I flee, but something other than the wall at my back held me in place. The box. The same one that had held the sword.

"Ah, Ms. O'Meara. We've been looking for you." The auctioneer's smile widened as he came to a stop before me. "Your proxy asked us to deliver this to you directly."

"My proxy?" I squeaked, taking a step back even as he presented the wooden box in outstretched arms.

"Why, yes. She made sure to inform us of your desire to get the artefact to safety as soon as possible. Most understandable, given your unbelievably generous donation."

He nodded at the box expectantly, and despite my better judgement, I reached forward and lifted the lid. I snapped it closed with a sharp inhale. Yep. I wasn't going crazy. That was definitely the sword in there.

"Would you like our security to escort you to your vehicle?" the auctioneer asked, relinquishing the box to my custody.

I tensed, shaking my head quickly as I eyed the three security guards. "No need. Honestly."

Apparently satisfied with my response, the auctioneer bowed his head in acknowledgement and bid me farewell. To my surprise, the guards followed him away without argument.

"What the hell just happened?" I turned to Bres, confusion a complete understatement for what I was feeling as I stood there dumbly holding the wooden box.

His mouth turned down in a scowl as he scanned the room, clearly looking for something – or someone. "If I had to guess, I'd say the sword is needed for the ritual. Bannon clearly set this up so that it would be in your possession when the time comes."

"That doesn't make sense. If he wanted me to have it, why not just courier it to me? Why all this?" I indicated to the still-crowded ballroom, my brow scrunching. Surely there was no need for this spectacle if the end goal was simply to give me the sword.

"Why waste the opportunity to further..." Bres trailed off as his gaze locked on something across the room.

I turned to follow his line of sight and spotted the three Watchers pushing their way through the crowd towards us. My hands tightened involuntarily on the box in my arms.

"The Watchers will take it from you," Bres warned, an edge of urgency in his voice as he turned his body to once more block mine. "I can keep it safe. Let me get it out of here for you, Aisling. I know you don't trust me, but I promise I can keep it out of their hands until you've had time to decide what you want to do."

The pleading in his eyes almost broke me. He was right that the idea of the Watchers taking the sword didn't sit well with me, but we'd been down this road far too many times. I was long past the fool-me-twice phase, and I couldn't do it again.

"I'm sorry." I shook my head. "I want to trust you, but too much has happened."

His shoulders slumped in resignation, and there was a sadness in his eyes as he gave a single nod of acceptance. For a moment he seemed to be almost memorising my features, then he turned and began to walk away.

Something inside me demanded that I stop him, that I not let him leave like this. So, without thinking, I blurted the question that was burning in my mind. "Who was she? The woman in your notes?"

His steps faltered. He didn't look back at me as he answered, but his quiet words reached me nonetheless.

"My mother. Saoirse."

And with that, he was gone, leaving me staring at his retreating back, more confused than ever.

"Where the hell have you been?"

I whirled at the sound of Kate's voice and found the three Watchers had managed to cross the ballroom while I'd been distracted by Bres. Looked like my time to consider other options was gone.

"We've been trying to get into the VIP area all evening," Richie chimed in accusingly. "We finally get past the damn security to find you're not even there."

While he continued his rant, Kate's eyes landed on the box in my arms. "What's that?"

I swallowed, once more tightening my grip on the artefact. There was no point lying since I could hardly hide the bloody thing in my pocket, but I suddenly wished I'd taken more time to consider Bres's offer.

"It's the sword that was auctioned off. I've been informed that I purchased it by proxy."

The air shifted as the three Watchers' expressions became instantly unreadable. I had to resist the urge to fidget nervously under their scrutiny, but dammit, I hadn't done anything wrong.

Eamonn stepped forward and reached to take the box from me. "We should get this back to HQ."

I hesitated, not wanting to hand it over, but not wanting to make a scene either. Kate, seeming to sense this, gave a subtle shake of her head and Eamonn stepped back. We all knew that wasn't going to be the end of it, however, so it cost them nothing to humour me.

Kate beckoned for me to follow and we began to make our way out of the large ballroom where people still mingled, discussing the events of the past hour. We'd reached the large double doors when a figure on the far side of the room caught my attention. Declan Bannon raised a glass of champagne in my direction, and even from a distance I could see his smile of satisfaction. A chill washed over me, and I shivered.

Nobody stopped us as we retrieved the car and made our swift exit from the venue. I wasn't sure whether or not to be grateful for that fact.

The drive to the Watchers HQ was uncomfortably silent. I had no doubt that the others had questions about the sword and why it was in my possession. Pity I had no more answers than they did. Unease rolled through me as Kate drove up the long road that led to the HQ. When she continued around the side of the building to an entrance I'd never seen before, that unease only grew.

She killed the engine and twisted in her seat to look at me. "Brian is waiting to speak to us inside."

Silently, I climbed out of the car, keeping hold of the box in my arms as I did. I wasn't naïve enough to believe I'd be walking back out of here with the sword, and something inside me railed at the idea of giving it up. What was it with this damn artefact?

I trailed behind Kate as she led me through what looked like a fire exit and down a dark corridor. Richie and Eamonn took up the rear, and I wondered how much of that was coincidence or to make sure I didn't bolt. We came to another door, and she pushed it open to reveal a small meeting room. Unlike the other meeting rooms I'd been in, this one was hard and uninviting. Plastic chairs surrounded a wooden table and the only light came from the harsh fluorescent lights.

Brian was already waiting inside the room as we entered, and with him was a familiar face that I hadn't expected to see. Maggie, the scientist who had been in charge of Teagan's so-called training was at his side, her hands clasped in front of her and an expectant look on her face.

"Aisling," Brian said, giving the box in my arms only the briefest of glances. "Maggie here will take the sword. We have facilities here to ensure it is properly contained."

Though I'd known this was likely to happen, the fact that he wanted me to hand it over to *her* was more than I could stomach. I opened my mouth to protest, but the other three Watchers closed in behind me, the message clear.

Against the screaming protest from every fibre of my being, I handed the wooden box to Maggie. "Are you planning to test this on some lab rats too?"

"If it will help us understand its nature better, then yes."

With that, she turned and left the room. The heavy door shut behind her with a solid clunk, and I knew I wouldn't be walking out of here any time soon.

CHAPTER TEN

Brian gestured for me to take a seat as my three babysitters placed themselves at the end of the table closest to the door. The plastic chair scraped against the floor as I pulled it out.

"Why did the Order give you the sword?"

With a weary sigh, I shrugged. "How the hell should I know?"

"It seems convenient, don't you think, that you failed to mention the Order had previously extended an invitation to this event? And then for you to be miraculously gifted with the very same artefact we sent you there to observe..."

I tensed. How did he know about the Order's invitation?

"In case you've forgotten," I said, my tone calm despite the sudden desire to punch him in the face, "I was only there on your instruction. When the Order approached me, I made it clear where they could shove their invitation. *You* put me in that room tonight, not me."

"So you expect us to believe that somebody funded a five million euro bid out of the kindness of their heart to give you a present?"

I gaped at him, dumbstruck. "No. I expect you to believe that the Order –"

A sharp rap on the door cut off my words, and Maggie stepped back into the room. She held what looked like a small white card in her hand as she made a beeline for Brian. The two spoke in voices too low for me to hear, but I was pretty sure from the glances in my direction that I was the subject of conversation.

Brian turned to me as Maggie once more left the meeting room. He held up the card that she must have passed him at some point during their conversation. "It appears that the Order took the opportunity to send you a message with the sword, Ms. O'Meara."

I frowned in confusion and took the card he held out to me.

You're going to need this. Bring sword and the ritual to the old HQ in three days' time. Noon.

The floor seemed to disappear from beneath me, and I clenched the edge of the table to stop myself from falling. Bres had been right – the sword was needed for the Claiming ritual. And if the Order expected me to bring them the details of the ritual in three days' time, it could only mean they intended to complete it sooner rather than later.

Brian watched my reaction closely. My shock was

clearly enough to convince him I wasn't a willing player in this game, though in truth, I didn't give a shit about his opinion right now.

He pulled out the chair across from me and sat down, clasping his hands in front of him. "The Order want you to complete the Claiming ritual for them. I have another proposal for you."

Wariness replaced shock, and I tensed, waiting for the inevitable shoe to drop.

"Though you may not be working with the Order, we both know you've been keeping information from us regarding their intentions to complete the Claiming. We also both know that you don't trust me or the Watchers." He leaned back in his chair and let that sit for a moment between us. "I want to change that. I want us to work together, as we should have been from the beginning. We have a wealth of historical information available here, and we're happy to place that at your disposal. Work with us to stop the Order."

I was pretty sure I was doing a great fish impersonation as I opened and closed my mouth, lost for words. He wasn't wrong about me keeping information from him, but there was definitely an element of pot, kettle, black going on here. However, since I actually wanted to get out of this place at some point, I decided it was best not to point that out.

"What are you suggesting?"

Brian gestured to the paper still gripped tightly in my hand. "I think we can safely assume from the

Order's note that the alignment required for the ritual will be happen sooner rather than later."

"You mean, you don't already know the timeline?" So much for their wealth of knowledge.

"We have our suspicions," Brian conceded. "But without the ritual, we can't be certain."

"Okay, then how about I find out the timeline for you? You guys stop the Order from completing the ritual, and I'll take a holiday so I'm not getting in your way." I was only half joking with the suggestion, though I had no doubt Brian would prefer I was out of the picture full stop, despite his olive branch.

He raised an eyebrow. "But your presence is required, is it not?"

Unease prickled over my skin. "My presence would only be required if the ritual was going ahead. Surely my absence would be more beneficial in this case."

Silence hung heavy between us as Brian assessed me, seeming to consider his next words carefully. I already knew I wasn't going to like them.

"We don't believe it's possible to stop the Claiming," he said finally. "The Order have been in control of the board for too long. They won't let the opportunity pass them by." He leaned forward, his eyes burning with determination. "The only way we can hope to win is by committing to the game."

I swallowed hard, my throat tightening. "What exactly are you suggesting? Because I don't know about you, but I really don't want Bannon as my magical overlord."

Brian's lips twitched and for a terrifying moment, I thought he was actually going to smile. I wasn't sure I could cope with that kind of shift in status quo right now.

"I think that's something we can actually agree on – for a change. My proposal is simple. The Watchers of Danu have existed as long as the Order and are best placed in terms of information and resources for the new reality we all find ourselves in. We want you to complete the Claiming. But we want you to do it for *us*."

The air suddenly seemed to get sucked out of the room and my head began to spin. They wanted me to what?

"Are you shitting me?" I stared at him, waiting for the punchline of what had to be the world's worst joke.

"The magic needs to be protected. There are people out there who would seek to abuse it, and I'm not just referring to the Order. The Watchers have the means and knowledge to do that."

Oh my god, he was actually serious.

I struggled to wrap my mind around the realisation even as alarm bells blared in my head.

"We're not interested in stripping you of your title, of course. You'd still be the Guardian. But the future we have ahead of us is treacherous. It's only a matter of time before magic becomes common knowledge. We can help guide people through that and ensure it is managed and controlled in the best possible way."

The eyes of all four Watchers in the room pressed

down on me, and I was suddenly very aware of my surroundings. Brian wouldn't be naïve enough to believe I'd jump at this suggestion, but would he let me walk out of here if he realised the true extent of my opposition?

Carefully schooling my expression, I pretended to – reluctantly – consider what he was saying. "How can I trust that what you're saying is true and the Watchers don't just want the power for themselves?"

Far from being insulted by my question, Brian gave me an approving nod. "It's a fair question. And I've no doubt that any answer I give you will be construed as a lie until you're ready to trust us. So, I simply ask you – what is your alternative?"

The question hit almost like a physical blow. He was right and we both knew it; my options were terrifyingly few right now. I wanted the Watchers to take ownership of the magic about as much as I wanted the Order to – which was not at all. But what chances did I truly have of stopping both of them? An utter sense of helplessness washed over me, bringing with it a searing anger. I was so sick of being a pawn in other people's games.

Working hard to keep my thoughts from showing, I gave an apologetic shrug. "Even if I wanted to help you, we don't have the ritual."

"We have people working on that. We've already deduced that the ritual needs to be completed during a rare moment in time and have narrowed down a few options. The Order's note now helps us pinpoint the most likely event. Given our extensive research capabilities, I'm confident we will have the answers we need soon."

He no doubt meant the comment to be reassuring. Instead, my apprehension ratcheted up about twenty knots. I needed to get out of here so I could think clearly without my every reaction being scrutinised.

Chewing my lip, I debated my options. "You've given me a lot to think about. I need some time to consider what you've said," I hedged.

I held my breath, waiting for the show of camaraderie to end and the command to lock me up. It didn't come. Brian simply nodded.

"That is to be expected. Of course, time is running short so your expediency would be appreciated." He stood as if to escort me out, and I was pretty sure shock was written all across my face.

"I meant what I said, Aisling. I want us to work together. Magic has the potential to do great things in our world, but it also has the potential to destroy us. We want to make sure that doesn't happen."

CHAPTER ELEVEN

Kate dropped me back at Teagan's apartment without saying a word. I was grateful she didn't try to push me for my thoughts on Brian's proposal, and even more grateful to be out of the Watchers HQ. Exhaustion had settled in every part of my body as the adrenaline from the night finally wore off. When I climbed out of the car and spotted amber eyes watching me from the shadows, I didn't even have the energy to trigger the fight-or-flight response that was often my instinctive reaction to seeing Pete's wolf.

I waited until Kate drove off before turning to him. "Hey. Were you just waiting for me, or is there some new Big Bad I need to worry about?"

Please let it be the first one. I really wanted to get these damned stilettos off me and climb into bed.

The large brown wolf stepped from the shadows and came to bump his nose against my hand. I gave his head an affectionate rub, and we made our way to the entrance of the apartment block together.

"You coming up?" I asked, stopping at the door. I wasn't sure if werewolves were included in the no-pets policy, but I doubted anyone would be brave enough to say anything.

The wolf gave a slight shake of his head and nudged me again with his nose. I gave him a small wave and made my way inside.

Teagan had the door to the apartment open before I even had a chance to dig my keys out of the tiny purse I was carrying. She pulled me inside, holding me at arm's length as she scanned me from head to toe for any sign of damage.

"I'm okay," I assured her. "Just tired."

"We were worried when you weren't back sooner. Pete was going out to see if he could track you."

I dropped onto the sofa, swiftly divesting myself of the torture devices I'd been calling shoes for the night. "I met his wolf outside. He must have been heading out just as Kate dropped me off. The Watchers felt the need to interrogate me after the auction."

Teagan's eyes bugged out of her head. "What?" She held up a hand. "Actually, hold that thought. I've a feeling this calls for some wine."

She had a glass of Pinot in both our hands within less than a minute. Settling onto the sofa next to me, she fixed her full attention on me. "Okay, fill me in."

So, I brought her up to speed on everything, from Bres's appearance to the sword to Brian's shocking proposal. Her eyes darkened with concern, and it was almost a relief to know my own fears weren't unfounded.

"But all that is a problem for tomorrow me." I turned my attention to the open books spread haphazardly across the living room floor and looked at Teagan in question. "Anything?"

She sighed. "Not much. I think I might be able to pinpoint the timeline based on what the Order's note indicates, but the dreamscape..." She shook her head. "There doesn't seem to be much on the collapse of magical realms."

I choked out a laugh, a lump lodging in my throat as I was once again reminded that the Claiming wasn't the only thing I needed to worry about. The last of my wine disappeared in one large gulp that did little to provide comfort.

Standing, I gave her a tired smile and gestured to my face. "I'm going to take this crap off and head to bed. I want to check in on Killian and make sure he's doing okay."

Teagan reached out and gave my hand a squeeze. I couldn't help but examine her eyes for any sign of that telltale purple colour.

"Hey, anymore on the plans for your great-grandmother to visit?"

A smile lit my friend's face. "Soon, hopefully. I was talking to her this evening and she was getting some things in place so she could come spend a bit of time here."

"Do you need me to move out for a bit? I can go stay at my mam's." Even if the thought sounded like torture, the last thing I wanted to do was make it hard for Teagan to get to know her family.

But my friend waved away my suggestion. "I'll organise a hotel nearby for her. As much as I'm excited to spend more time getting to know her, it's still very early days. We'll both need our space."

I nodded, though I couldn't help the niggle of worry that I was overstaying my welcome. As soon as all this madness with the Claiming was over, I was going to have to find a way out of the job with the Watchers and get something more reliable that could go on a mortgage application without raising awkward questions.

With yet another worry added to my ever-growing list, I bid Teagan goodnight and made my way to my room. Sleep took me almost as soon as my head hit the pillow. Darkness embraced me, slow and reluctant to relinquish its hold. Finally though, the dreamscape materialised around me and I found myself in the centre of the meadow, sitting on a blanket of green grass that was now looking scorched in places.

With a sense of foreboding, I looked up.

Part of me had fervently hoped the crack in the sky had been little more than my imagination and would be gone next time I came here. That hope was instantly shattered. Not only was the jagged crack still there, but now further cracks spiderwebbed from its centre extending outwards. The sky had taken on an unsettling grey hue that warned of storms to come, and the soothing warmth of the sun was noticeably absent again. I didn't waste any time dwelling on the changes, however. Something told me I didn't have that luxury.

I got to my feet and headed for the tree line. Determination drove my steps as I traversed the path to Killian's stone cottage from memory. This time, the heavy wooden door stood ajar, as if awaiting my arrival.

I rapped gently on the frame. "Killian?"

Given the dull grey of the dreamscape, the daylight that filtered into the cottage did little to penetrate the darkness, and it took my eyes a moment to adjust.

Killian was where I had last seen him, on the makeshift bed in the corner of the room. He was sitting this time and aware of my presence, but his eyes looked sunken and there was no mistaking the exhaustion in every line of his body.

"Hey." I moved to sit next to him on the bed, careful not to jostle him.

"I wasn't sure if you'd come back."

Frowning, I turned my body to make sure I had his full attention so he could see how sincere I was. "Of course I was going to come back. I told you I'm going to help you, and I meant it."

He reached up a hand to cup my cheek but dropped it, the limb seeming almost too heavy for him to hold up for long. "This is the way things were meant to be. You have more important things that need your attention right now."

"You mean the Claiming."

When I'd first broached the topic of the Claiming with Killian, he'd shut me down immediately, refusing to even acknowledge it, let alone speak to me about it. The fact that he was now willing to discuss it brought a whole new sense of fear.

"You can't let the Order complete the ritual."

"Well, no shit, Sherlock. I'm guessing that goes for the Watchers too?"

Killian frowned. "The Watchers? What do you mean?"

"Oh, you know. They apparently believe they should be the ones to Claim magic so they can keep us little people safe from it. Or it safe from us. I'm not too sure which. Either way, I'm not a fan of their suggestion."

His expression was grim as he nodded. "I'd be inclined to agree. Even the best intentions can become warped by power, and Claiming the land's magic is a power unlike anything you can fathom."

The now all-too-familiar sense of panic tightened my chest as I considered the extent of what I was facing. "I don't know if I'm strong enough to stop them," I admitted quietly.

I waited for the condemnation to come. I was the Guardian; it was my job to keep the magic safe, and I'd already failed in every way possible. But Killian didn't say anything. He just reached over and took my hand in his.

Though his grip still had enough strength to be

reassuring, his skin was cold, and I was once more aware of his increasing frailty compared to the man I'd first met here in the dreamscape. He was fading away, and I had no idea how much longer he could hold back the dark magic.

"What if there's a third option?" I blurted before I could really think about it.

Killian's brow furrowed in confusion.

"Bres wants me to be the one to Claim the magic," I explained, my words hurried as I tried to make sense of the thought that had been playing on my mind. "He wants to stop the Order and thinks it's the only way to keep the magic from them. I don't want the magic, but I sure as hell don't want the Order or the Watchers to have it. What if he's right, and this is the only way to do that? I'm the Guardian. I'm meant to be protecting it. Plus, if I did Claim it, maybe it would give me the strength I need to help you, to keep you safe from whatever the hell is happening to the dreamscape."

The hand holding mine tensed as Killian grew deathly still. "No," he said, no room for argument or debate in that one single word.

"Do you think I'd abuse the power?" I tried to ignore the sting of hurt at the idea he might think such a thing.

He shook his head. "No, I don't believe that for a second. But Bres can't be trusted, Aisling. You need to take my word on this."

"I already know he's not suggesting this from the goodness of his heart," I protested. "He's even told me himself that his sole motivation is to stop the Order from getting what they want. That doesn't mean it's not worth considering."

"He wants to destroy the magic."

I reared back. "Destroy the... What do you mean?"

"Bres's ancestor wanted to destroy magic. He knew that during the Claiming ritual, the balance would be at its most unstable. He was encouraging the Fomorians to complete the ritual so he could turn on them when they, and the magic, were at their most vulnerable. I believe Bres is planning the same thing."

Words failed me and I shook my head in denial. But something about what Killian said rang true to me, and I found it impossible to argue.

Bres wanted revenge. And what would be a better revenge – to hand the magic the Order wanted to somebody else and leave the door open for them to reclaim it, or to destroy it entirely?

My mouth went dry as a sinking feeling told me I'd been played. Again.

Killian slumped back against the wall behind him, exhaustion seeming to take hold of him once more. "Besides," he said, "it wouldn't change things anyway. In order for the Claiming to be completed, all the magic needs to return to your world. The very act of completing the ritual will destroy this plane of existence."

CHAPTER TWELVE

The cold light of day seeped into my consciousness, bringing with it a chilling sense of dread. Killian. The dreamscape. The Claiming. It all seemed so immense and the problems so insurmountable that I didn't even know where to begin.

Killian hadn't said in so many words that he would cease to exist once the dreamscape did, but I was more than able to read between the lines.

Wanting nothing more than to bury my head under the covers and pretend it was all just a bad dream, I forced myself to sit up and face facts. The Order's invitation was a ticking time bomb and none of this was magically going away. I needed to start getting answers. And first up – I needed to know if it was actually possible to destroy magic.

I reached for my ancestor's book where it rested on my bedside locker and settled myself into a comfortable cross-legged position on the bed. Then I took a moment to close my eyes and say a silent prayer that I'd find a nice, simple answer for once in this whole damned mess. You know, something like a handy little paragraph confirming that it was impossible to destroy magic.

It wasn't that I believed Killian to be way off base with his theory. I just couldn't reconcile the thought of something so horrible with who I believed Bres to be deep down; his regular betrayals aside, he wasn't evil. Not truly.

I flicked through the pages, not quite sure what I was looking for other than information to help put my mind at ease. When I came across notes on energy and how it manifested in our world, I stopped. Did magic count as a form of energy? I guessed so.

Energy is malleable. It can be changed and mutated until it becomes almost unrecognisable from its original form. This is the essence of what we are doing with our magic, and so we must not underestimate the responsibility that comes with such an ability. For while energy will never cease to be, it can become corrupted to an extent that it may become unusable – or highly volatile.

A shiver ran down my spine at the ominous warning.

It seemed I had found the reassurance I'd been seeking, and it wasn't in fact possible to destroy magic. But corrupt it? Change it until it became unrecognisable, almost useless? That was close enough to the same thing – and could even be worse if the book's warning was anything to go by.

Subconsciously my hands drifted down to rest on my belly where the comforting warmth of my magic resided. The brief time I'd been without it after Carmen used the cauldron to drain me had really brought it home to me how much I'd come to rely on its presence. No, I wasn't slinging spells about like a pro, but I was so much more attuned to the world around me than ever before. I didn't want to lose that again.

With a resigned sigh, I pulled out the photocopies of Bres's notes from where I'd shoved them under my bed. I already knew what they contained, but now that I had a context for who Saoirse was, I couldn't help but hope that I'd be able to gleam some new understanding from them. Something that would help me determine if Killian's fears were truly justified.

As with the last time I looked through them, I only found Saoirse mentioned once, in an entry dated almost twenty years ago. It detailed the first time Bres was called upon to help the Order acquire a rare artefact – not by wholly legal means. By my best estimations, he'd have probably been about eleven or twelve at the time, and it made me sad to think of such a young boy being dragged into that life.

The only mention of Saoirse had been a reference to how upset she'd been when she found out. Reading it now, I realised that the change in tone I'd previously noticed was most likely driven by his shame. Nobody ever wanted to disappoint their mother, and I doubted Bres was any different.

What had it been like for him growing up as part of the Order? The impression I got – from that brief reference, at least – was that his mother didn't want him involved with their activities. So, why had they stayed?

Curious to learn more, I brought up the browser on my phone. Hazarding a guess that she shared the same last name as Bres, I tried searching her name. The first thing that came up was a death notice.

I sucked in a breath.

Saoirse Ann Donoghue. Loving mother of Bres Donoghue. Born 6th May 1971. Died 10th December 2003.

That was only a few months after the diary entry I'd been reading. God, he'd been so young when she died.

An aching sadness swelled in my chest. No child should have to face losing a parent that young. As much as my mam drove me insane, I couldn't imagine a world without her in it. And that age was already such a confusing time without the emotional toll of such a loss.

I scanned for any additional information that might give me insight into the woman who raised Bres. Halfway down the list, a newspaper article dated the same day as the death notice caught my eye.

Mother of one in suicide tragedy.

With a trembling hand, I opened the article and read. By the time I got to the end, tears burned the back of my eyes.

What could be bad enough to drive someone to

take their own life? How could she have left her young child?

Nothing I could find on the internet was going to answer those questions for me. And really, it didn't matter. Whatever drove her to do it, I knew deep down that this was the answer I needed. If Bres believed the Order played some part in his mother's suicide, it would be more than sufficient motivation for him to destroy magic. Hell, if I was in his shoes, I'd probably feel the same.

Unfortunately for him, I couldn't allow it to happen. Regardless of the ache of sorrow that filled me on his behalf, I knew at the very core of my being that I had to protect the magic. No matter the cost.

Wiping tears from my cheeks, I took a shuddery breath and rose. It was time to face whatever the day had in store for me. Good or bad.

By the time I emerged from my bedroom, Teagan was already engrossed in research. She looked up from the texts and files she had spread out around her on the living room floor and frowned.

"You okay?"

I slumped down on the ground next to her, not quite sure how to answer. "Find anything?" I asked instead.

She pulled a large tome with a black leather cover closer to us and opened it to a page she had book-marked. "I've been trying to confirm our theory about the timing of the ritual being linked to a rare lunar event. I figured it would have to be something particularly rare, or the Order would have been pestering you months ago. And given their demand for you to hand over the ritual in a couple of days, I'm guessing it's something that's coming soon."

I looked down at the page she'd opened. Lunar eclipses and their definitions. Sounded like fun bedtime reading.

Some of the terms were familiar enough to me, but I'd never known there were so many eclipse variations. I had no idea what it was I was supposed to be focusing on, but thankfully, Teagan took pity on me.

"According to news reports, we're due to have a triple lunar eclipse," she said, pointing to one of the items halfway down the list.

"And that is?"

She shrugged. "Pretty much what it says on the tin. Three eclipses in a short space of time. A solar, a lunar, and another solar eclipse. Apparently, two are common enough over the course of a month, but three in a row are really rare. Astronomers are wetting themselves over it."

My knowledge of astronomy was up there with my knowledge of chemistry – pretty much non-existent – so I had no idea if this was significant enough to be what we were looking for. But it was our best clue to date.

"Do we know when it's due to happen?"

Teagan pulled up the calendar on her phone. "The first solar eclipse is expected about a week from now, with the lunar eclipse two weeks after that, and the second solar eclipse two weeks after that."

I swallowed hard. Seven days from now?

"What are the chances that the ritual can't be done until the final eclipse?"

I didn't know which response was worse – Teagan's silence, or the worry that clouded her blue eyes.

CHAPTER THIRTEEN

I stood staring up at the apartment block where Bres lived and debated with myself, as I had for the past twenty minutes, whether or not to go in. Even being here was stupid. I knew that. Yet, try as I might, I hadn't been able to convince myself to walk away.

Knowing now what I did about his mother, I found myself even more compelled to get through to Bres. Nobody could blame him for his desire for revenge, but I knew deep down that if he succeeded in destroying magic, it would also destroy the final bit of good in him. I really didn't want that to happen.

With a sigh, I turned away. Who was I kidding? He wasn't going to listen to me. I was wasting my time.

"Are you planning on standing around here all day, or were you going to come up at some point?"

I jumped at the sound of Bres's voice behind me. Heat burned my cheeks as I spun around to find him leaning against the entryway, one eyebrow cocked as he watched me. He was back in his casual jeans and t-shirt but still looked as good as he had at the auction. Without the mask covering part of his face, I could see the bruising hadn't yet faded entirely, and I wondered again what other cruelties he'd suffered at the hands of the Order.

"I hadn't decided," I muttered. Did it come out somewhat petulant? Yes, it did. But I was irritated with myself for letting him catch me unawares.

Unfazed by my attitude, he nodded as if the answer made perfect sense. "Okay. Well, I'm going to grab a coffee, and then you can let me know what you've decided."

I didn't miss the amusement that sparkled in his blue eyes as he turned and disappeared into the coffee shop next door to his apartment block. He emerged again a couple of minutes later with two cups in his hand. He held one out to me.

"Coconut hot chocolate with chocolate flakes and extra marshmallows. Promise it's not poisoned."

My heart gave a traitorous flutter as he offered me my favourite drink. He'd seen me drink it before; the fact he'd thought of ordering it for me meant nothing. I wrapped my two hands around the cup, seeking comfort from its warmth as I tried to tell myself I truly believed that.

"Walk with me?"

I nodded and followed Bres as he crossed the road and headed down the path that ran along the River Liffey. For a few minutes, we walked in silence. The city was bustling with people going about their daily lives, and I tried to remember exactly what that level of blissful ignorance felt like.

"Did they take it? The Watchers," Bres clarified when I looked at him in confusion. "Did they take the sword?"

I hesitated, not sure exactly how much to say or not say. Eventually, I settled for, "It's safe."

Sure, that might have been a lie since I had no idea what the Watchers were doing with it, but given the sword was likely connected to the Claiming ritual, vague seemed like the best option.

Silence fell between us once more and I debated how to broach the topic of his mother. It seemed insensitive to ask about her, but he'd told me himself that she was the driving force behind his need for revenge, so...

"What was she like? Your mother."

Bres glanced sideways at me, his surprise quickly masked by a carefully schooled expression. When he finally answered though, there was a softness to his tone that I wasn't used to hearing from him.

"She was ... beautiful. When I was young and I had nightmares, she'd climb into bed beside me and tell me stories of magical lands where the heroes always won." He gave a bitter laugh. "She was too good for this world. Especially one where the Order was making the rules. But she had a fierce heart and did everything she could to shield me from that reality."

It hadn't been enough though; I didn't need to hear the unspoken words to know that.

"What age were you when she died?"

"Thirteen."

"So young," I whispered. My heart ached for him, for the young boy he'd been, and for the man he could be now if things had been different.

"You don't stay young for long when you grow up as part of the Order. Though you probably already gathered that from the notes you copied."

My steps faltered. It was an effort not to look up and see if there was a neon "guilty" sign flashing above my head. Apparently I hadn't been as stealthy as I'd thought with my sneaky photography.

I decided to take a leaf out of his book and simply ignore the comment. "She didn't approve of what the Order were doing?"

He shook his head, his jaw visibly clenching. "She tried to shield me from it, but Bannon only let her get away with that until I was old enough to be of use to him."

He turned to look out over the Liffey, and his grip tightened on the paper cup in his hand. "She was so disappointed the first time I agreed to do a job for him. She begged me not to do it, but I wanted Bannon's approval so much – not for me, for her, so that her life would be better, so that people would stop treating her like something they scraped off their shoe." He blew out a shaky breath and ran a hand through his hair.

"Why didn't she leave? Why didn't she take you and get as far away from the Order as possible?"

"The Order's reach extends further than you could ever imagine. Bannon made sure we had everything we needed, but we had nothing of our own. Even if she hadn't known they'd come after us, she had no means to provide for us."

He shrugged. "It wasn't all bad. When I was a kid, she'd invent these adventures for us to share. I can still remember how her face would light up with excitement when we went hunting for buried treasure or to find mystical lost lands. For a long time, I didn't even realise that my life was different than other kids."

"You mean because of the Order?"

"We were never part of the Order, not really. Our bloodline, the continued link to the Tuatha was necessary, but not welcomed. The older I got, the more it bothered me, how they made us outcasts, made her feel less than. So, when the chance came to prove myself useful, I was determined to show them exactly what I was capable of."

"And did you?" Of course, I already knew he'd been successful in his first job, but now that he was talking so openly, I was reluctant to let him stop.

"Oh, yeah. I pulled off something that even experienced members of the Order would've struggled to do. I was so proud. Then I saw my mother's reaction when I told her. I'll never forget the expression on her face. She was heartbroken. And it was all because of me."

My throat tightened, and without thinking, I

reached out to put a hand on his arm. I wanted to wrap my arms around him and hold him, to tell him that it was okay, that he'd been a child, and that I was sorry for everything he'd gone through. But I didn't, and after a moment, I dropped my hand.

"The next time Bannon asked me to do a job," he continued, his tone taking on a dull, emotionless edge, "I refused. As much as I wanted to make things better for us, I couldn't bear seeing that look on her face again."

"What happened?" I asked softly. Because there was no way Bannon simply took no for an answer when he wanted something.

"I found her that evening. Bannon had me on cleaning duty, no doubt as punishment for refusing, though he never explicitly said it. When I got back to our apartment ... she was just lying there. The pills were scattered across the floor, but still it took me a minute to understand why she wasn't blinking. I kept calling her name, expecting her to answer."

Oh god, he'd been the one to find her. I covered my mouth with my hand, swallowing hard.

"Our favourite book was open on the floor beside her. The pages were flipped to the very end, and she'd written 'I'm sorry' underneath the final sentence."

"Oh, Bres."

He stopped walking and turned to me. "I know what you're thinking. How could she have done it? How could she have left her son like that?"

I shook my head but couldn't make myself speak

the denial aloud because he was right; it didn't make sense to me. Especially not after everything he had told me about her.

"She didn't kill herself."

He made the statement so simply, so void of emotion, that it caught me off guard.

"What do you mean?"

"It was a message. From Bannon. He wanted me to understand what happened when I defied him. He wanted me to know that I had no free will other than what he allowed me to have."

A sinking horror settled over me as his words caused pieces of the puzzle to click into place. His theory made so much sense, and yet I didn't want to believe that anybody could be capable of something so evil. Not even Bannon.

"How can you be sure?"

"She'd never have left me there alone with them. She might have hated the Order, but she loved me. I know what the newspapers said, but they were wrong."

Bres reached out and gripped my free hand, my hot chocolate long-forgotten in the other. "So now you know. Now you know the real reason why I want – no, *need* – to make them pay. Please, Aisling. Please help me."

My chest ached, and I wanted nothing more than to take the pain from his eyes, to be able to offer the help he sought. But I couldn't, especially not if Killian's theory was true. Whether he realised it or not, destroying magic wouldn't bring him peace. I'd be damned if I let him sacrifice any more than the Order had already taken from him.

"She wouldn't want this for you." I gripped his hand tightly, willing him to understand. "She'd want you to be happy, not building your whole life around this need for revenge."

He released his hold on my hand and stepped back, his expression becoming shuttered. "You won't help me."

I shook my head, sorrow pressing against my chest with a force that felt like my ribs might shatter. "I'm sorry, Bres. I can't."

CHAPTER FOURTEEN

Bres let me walk away without any argument, but the guilt stayed with me through the night and well into the following day. By the time I met up with Teagan and Pete back at the apartment to discuss a plan of action, I was exhausted from the weight of everything pressing down on me.

It was day three, the day the Order had instructed me to bring the ritual to them. Of course, that was never going to happen even if we'd managed to uncover it. Since we'd gotten no further than possibly narrowing down the timeline, they wouldn't be able to take the information from me by force either – something I had no doubt they'd be willing to do.

"I want to go to the meeting." Pete paced the length of the living room as he made the absurd declaration.

He'd been following the same path for long enough now that I half expected to see the carpet wearing away. He was on edge. We all were.

Teagan's frown mirrored my own as we tore our attention from yet another pile of old mythology texts that Teagan had managed to "borrow" in the guise of running a research project with her students.

"We've already agreed that we're ignoring their request," I protested.

"Yes, but we also know they're not just going to take no for an answer." Pete finally stopped his pacing and turned to look at us, his jaw set in determination. "My wolf can go. So long as I stay hidden, they'll never even know I was there. I can follow whoever turns up. If we're lucky, they might lead me to the new base the Order is using."

Teagan shook her head. "And if we're unlucky, you'll get caught and get yourself killed."

A lump lodged in my throat at the thought, and I added my own objection to Teagan's. "It's too dangerous."

"It might give us an opportunity to find out where they're keeping the cauldron," he countered.

I sucked in a breath. That was a low blow. He knew how hard it was for me not to worry about the cauldron and what the Order were planning to do with the magic it contained. Which meant he also knew it would make me hesitate. But I wasn't naive enough to think we could get the cauldron from the Order a second time, even if we did know where they were keeping it.

"The Order won't be looking for a wolf," he pressed. "I'll stay out of sight and only follow if it's safe.

At the very least, it will give us advanced warning if they decide to come for you straight away, Aisling."

There was no mistaking the concern that shone in his brown eyes. Even before Pete's dormant werewolf genetics had been triggered, he'd been protective of those he loved. We might not be together romantically anymore, but I had no doubt he still cared greatly for me and felt compelled to protect me. I just didn't want to be the reason he got hurt again.

"Are you sure you can make it there and back without being seen?" Teagan asked.

I snapped my head around to look at her. "You can't seriously be encouraging this?"

She shrugged. "He makes a good point. The Order aren't going to be happy when you don't show. I'd rather have as much advance notice of their plans as possible."

Pete's grin couldn't be described as anything other than wolfish as he nodded in agreement. I sighed, defeated.

Before I could demand that we plan every iota of this stupid idea out to the second in the hopes of limiting the risk, my phone began to vibrate insistently. "Unknown number" flashed on the screen, and my stomach clenched.

Hesitantly, I answered the call.

"Aisling?"

I frowned, not immediately recognising the woman's voice. "Who is this?"

"It's Kate. I need your help. My niece, her magic is manifesting, and she's freaking out. It's not good."

The note of panic that edged the Watcher's voice was unmistakable and more than a little unsettling, given how normally calm and collected she seemed to be. Still, I didn't know exactly how she thought I could help, and with everything going on here...

"Shouldn't you call the Watchers?"

"There's no time. This is going to start attracting attention really fast. Please, Aisling, just get here as quickly as you can."

She rattled off an address and then hung up, leaving me staring at the phone.

The area she mentioned was a residential one, not too far from Teagan's apartment, and if Kate was right about attracting attention, we couldn't allow that to happen. Torn, I looked at my friends.

Teagan waved me away. "Go, deal with whatever that is. Me and Pete have got this." She gave him a stern look. "I won't let him leave here until we have a solid plan. I promise."

Still feeling uneasy, I grabbed my stuff and hurried down to the underground car park to get my car. All the while, I repeated the address Kate had given me over and over in my head to make sure I didn't forget it.

Traffic was thankfully light and I reached the housing estate in a little over ten minutes. As I pulled to a stop outside a red-brick semi-detached house, I looked for any signs of the emergency Kate had called about. Everything seemed calm, but as I climbed out of the car, the faint smell of smoke tickled my nose. It seemed to be coming from the rear of the property, so I bypassed the front door and made a beeline for the gate that stood open at the side of the house.

A small back garden came into view, and I spotted Kate in the far corner, standing with her back to me. She didn't seem to register my approach, her attention fixed on the young girl crouched on the ground a few feet away from her. The girl appeared to be maybe thirteen or fourteen. Her long brown hair hung in strings around her face, and the sports kit she wore was smudged with dirt. She was visibly shaking, but that was somewhat understandable given the ring of fire that kept flaring up in a circle around her.

Energy crackled over my skin as I slowed my steps. There was no doubt in my mind that the fire was magical in nature, and the last thing I wanted to do was spook anyone.

"Kate?"

As I drew next to the Watcher, I noticed the beads of sweat on her forehead and the tension that radiated through her entire body. Kate darted a sideways glance at me before returning her full focus to her niece.

"She doesn't know how to control it, and I can't get through to her. I've been trying to take the air from the flames, but the magic seems to be reacting to her emotions."

As if in response to her words, the flames dimmed, flickering for a moment like they might wink out. Then they flared again, even brighter this time.

I swallowed, thinking hard. My skill with elemental magic wasn't terrible, but if oxygen deprivation wasn't working for Kate, it was unlikely I'd do any better.

"Can you control water?" I asked, thinking back to the first time I'd met her and the frost that had spread from her touch. It was the element I found hardest to work with unless there was a significant source from me to pull from, but maybe she could draw some from the earth to douse the flame.

Kate shook her head. "I've tried it already. There's not enough close by and the house is locked up."

That ruled out water. Maybe –

The sound of approaching sirens echoed through the air, and the young girl's eyes widened in terror. I cursed under my breath. Of course, a fire wouldn't go unnoticed in an estate like this. Kate had been right; this could get bad really quick if we didn't get it under control.

There was only one thing I could think of that I was fairly confident would work. It was the last thing I wanted to do, but we were running out of time.

I didn't give myself time to second-guess my decision. I edged past Kate and crouched down as close as I dared to the flickering flame. Heat scorched my skin as I placed my two hands flat against the earth and attempted to paste a reassuring smile on my face.

"My name is Aisling, and I'm here to help you, okay? I understand how scary all of this must be, but we're going to get through this together."

The girl blinked, the first crack in her fear-filled expression I'd seen since arriving.

"Can you tell me your name?" I asked gently, trying with great effort to ignore the cloying smoke that was making my eyes water and my throat burn.

"Jessie."

Her response was so quiet that it was barely audible of over the flash of fire that followed. I flinched back but forced myself not to retreat.

"Okay, Jessie. I need you to do something for me. It's very simple, I just want you to look all around and start naming everything you can see, no matter how silly. Can you do that for me?"

A crease formed between her brows with her confusion as she nodded, but she did as I asked.

With Jessie distracted, I turned my attention inwards, narrowing my focus on the magic that rested at my centre. Where the energy crackling around me felt volatile and unfamiliar, my own power surged through my veins with an ease that felt almost natural now. For a moment, fear flared bright inside me, making me falter. I had used my siphoning powers only once since my magic had replenished, when my relaxing break away to Lakeview had proven more exciting than expected. I'd saved a man's life and proven that my gift didn't have to destroy. Still, the fear lingered.

The sound of approaching sirens grew louder and I knew we had minutes at most. So, I pushed away all doubts and closed my eyes.

"Kate," I said, keeping my voice calm and carefully controlled, "I'm going to need you to let go of your magic." I didn't want to risk siphoning anything from her if I could avoid it.

To my relief, the Watcher didn't waste time arguing. The air around me changed, though thankfully the fire didn't spread more than an inch or so outward without Kate's efforts to contain it. I latched onto the energy that fuelled it, and I called it to me.

The head rush was instantaneous. While Jessie's magic was still new and untrained, it had a wildness that gave it power. I dug my fingers into the earth and imagined sucking only the flames to me, leaving the young girl untouched. Warmth flowed from my fingers and up my arms.

My eyes flashed open just as the circle of fire winked out. I slumped to the ground, dropping my forehead to the warm earth and inhaling deeply in an attempt to stop the world spinning.

Kate bolted past me and grabbed Jessie into her arms. The young girl was a sobbing, snotty mess and she clung to her aunt, apologising over and over again. I hoped like hell the overflow of emotion didn't start up any more flames, but I couldn't think straight to issue a warning.

Footsteps pounded from the side of the house, and two firemen came skidding to a stop in the middle of the back garden. "Ladies, we got a report that there was a fire here?"

CHAPTER FIFTEEN

Thankfully, the firemen accepted Kate's explanation that Jessie had been performing a little breakup ritual that had gone awry. Given the scorch marks on the grass, we couldn't deny that there had been a fire, but once they were satisfied that the scene was secure, they left with just a stern warning to the teenager about the dangers of playing with fire.

More than once during all this, I caught Kate casting curious glances my way. I pointedly ignored them and kept my focus firmly on Jessie, lest her magic decide to make another untimely appearance.

When the two firemen had finally gone, Kate turned to me. "We need to get Jessie back to HQ. The sooner we can explain to her what's going on and help her get a handle on her power, the safer everyone around her will be."

Because the girl was a walking fire hazard. Sympathy caused my chest to ache. I knew how scary it was to find out about magic for the first time. I couldn't imagine how much harder that would be to deal with when puberty was added to the mix. But now that the immediate danger was gone, I was acutely aware that the Order's meeting time was drawing near and I needed to get back to Teagan and Pete.

"I actually need to –"

"No." Kate cut me off before I could finish uttering my excuse. "You have to come with us to make sure Jessie's magic stays under control. I don't know exactly what you did to stop that fire, but I don't want my car to turn into a fireball while I'm driving, so you're coming. No arguments."

When she put it like that, there was nothing I could say that wouldn't come across petty, so I nodded mutely.

Anxiety twisted my insides as I glanced at the time on my phone. Less than an hour until the Order's appointed meeting time. It was unlikely I'd make it to the Watchers HQ and back to Teagan's in that time. I could only hope that Teagan and Pete had everything under control.

Once we were on the road, I sent Teagan a message filling her in on what had happened. Despite me glaring at the phone for the entire drive, there was no response. Jessie fell asleep with her head resting on my shoulder and as I took in the lines of her face, I was struck by how young she truly was. Seeing her so vulnerable made it hard to regret the help I'd given, but an uncomfortable feeling settled in the pit of my stomach nonetheless.

When we reached the Watchers HQ a team was waiting. They ushered Kate and Jessie away, and from one blink to the next, I found myself standing alone in the reception area wondering how the hell I was going to get back to my car.

"Don't worry, they'll get her the help she needs."

I jumped at the sound of Eamonn's voice and spun around to find that the Watcher had somehow managed to sneak up on me when I wasn't paying attention. He grinned at my obvious surprise.

"Brian sent me to come get you. He wants a word."

I groaned inwardly. Given there wasn't much else I could do, I followed obediently as Eamonn led me through the winding passages of the HQ. Though the path we took was familiar to me, I noticed this time that there seemed to be more activity than normal in the building.

We passed an open door that revealed what looked like a small library. Three women and two men had set up camp around the wooden tables at its centre, their heads buried in books that looked almost as old as the book my ancestors left me.

Eamonn slowed his steps in line with mine, noticing my curiosity. "They're researching the Claiming. Unfortunately, this is one of those times that computers can't give us all the answers – much to my dismay." He gave me a wry grin. "Luckily, we have an extensive collection here that has been well preserved. I'm sure Brian would be happy to allow you access."

I wasn't quite so sure about that, but I kept the thought to myself as we continued on.

A couple of minutes later, we came to a stop outside Brian's office. The sound of raised voices came from behind the closed door, so I was surprised when Eamonn opened the door without bothering to knock.

Teagan stood in front of Brian's desk, hands planted on her hips and a glare that almost made me feel sorry for the Watcher who sat across from her. Of course there was another, slightly petty part of me that giggled at seeing Brian get a scolding. Until realisation hit me.

"What are you doing here?" I interjected as I rushed into the office. Where was Pete? Had something happened?

Teagan turned, her expression showing no surprise at my appearance, though that might have simply been because she wasn't ready to let go of her anger yet. "That's just what I was asking Brian."

To Brian's credit, he didn't flinch from the dagger look she shot him. He sat forward, placing his hands out in appeal. "I can only apologise for any worry this situation has caused. Our team was operating with the best intentions. I'm sure you can understand that."

I frowned as I looked between them. It was clear I had missed a whole chunk of context. "Teagan?"

Moving to her side, I placed a hand on her arm to

draw her attention to me. Tension radiated from her and my frown deepened.

She inhaled deeply and gave herself a little shake as if to let go of the anger.

"Maggie called me not long after you left. She said they'd been reviewing my test results and needed me to come in immediately."

"What?" I spun her to face me fully. "Are you okay? What's wrong?"

Teagan gave a wry laugh, but I didn't miss the fear that clouded her eyes. "Nothing, as it turns out. Maggie said they were worried my power was unstable and could be a danger to anyone around me. So, of course I came in. I've been here for the past hour letting them run their tests, and now I'm being told they made a mistake. That everything is fine."

Relief washed through me, but it was immediately soured by suspicion. Had Maggie hoped to scare Teagan into resuming their "training"? I wouldn't put it past the battle-axe. This time it was my turn to glare at Brian.

He met my accusing gaze head on. "Like I said, it was thankfully a mistake. I'm sure you can understand why we needed to err on the side of caution, however. And since you're both here, I was hoping we might catch up."

He gestured to the two seats on the far side of his desk. I glanced at Teagan, more than ready to walk out of here if that was what she wanted. But she sighed and took one of the offered seats.

"Have the Order reached out to you at all?" he asked once we were both settled.

I shook my head. "Aside from the note they left with the sword, they haven't made any attempts to contact me." I glanced at my watch. The meeting time had come and gone, and I itched to ask Teagan whether or not Pete had followed through on the plan. Given our present company, I kept my questions to myself.

"That's good," Brian said, leaning back in his chair. "As you know, we've had people working hard to uncover details of the Claiming. The ritual itself still eludes us, but we think we have narrowed down the timeline."

I stayed quiet, pasting an expression of innocent curiosity on my face as I pointedly avoided looking at Teagan.

"There is a rare lunar phenomenon this month," he continued. "A triple eclipse month. It means there will be a solar eclipse, followed by a lunar eclipse a couple of weeks after that, and then another solar eclipse a couple of weeks after that. We believe this is the timeline that the Order are aligning their plans to. And we should be working to it also."

It took an effort for me not to point out that I hadn't agreed to their insane plan to complete the Claiming. Instead, I decided to make the most of his chatty mood.

"If there are three separate eclipses, do you have any idea which is the target?"

"We're working to narrow that down. At this point,

we believe the most likely catalyst to be the third eclipse since that's what makes the phenomenon so rare."

So, at best we had a little over a month. At worst…

A hard rap on the door halted any further questions I had. The three of us turned just as Richie pushed open the door and stuck his head inside. "You're going to want to come with me. Pete has been hurt."

CHAPTER SIXTEEN

The three of us followed Richie along the winding path that led to the small hospital wing housed at the centre of the HQ. He'd refused to offer up any more details other than to confirm that Pete was okay. Given where we going, it was understandable that I wasn't going to take his words at face value.

Anxiety held me in its claws as we finally slowed to a stop at a small white room with a large viewing window. It was the same room where Pete had recovered after being kidnapped by the sons of Carmen, and as I looked in the window now to see a large brown wolf lying in the centre of the floor, my breath froze in my chest.

The wolf's legs twitched and his head moved, as if beginning to stir. I whirled on Richie. "What the hell happened?" I demanded.

"He got hit by a car."

"What?"

"We were monitoring the old Order HQ and spotted your friend here skulking around the shadows. Apparently the Order did too, because a black car came out of nowhere and drove straight for him. He doesn't seem badly hurt, but we had to knock him out to get him out of there safely."

"You tranq'd him?" Teagan gaped at Richie in disbelief, looking like she might actually lunge at him.

"Well, I was hardly going to drive back here with a wolf breathing down my neck," he retorted mulishly.

His argument was hard to fault, though I understood Teagan's anger. I tuned them both out as Pete's wolf began to stir in earnest. The large beast reared its head and then stumbled to its feet. Even from beyond the glass window, I could sense the agitation rolling from Pete as he turned to assess his surroundings for any threats.

"Open the door," I ordered.

Richie looked at me as if I'd grown a second head. "D'ye not think you should give him a chance to come round properly first?"

"He won't hurt me." I moved to the door and looked at him expectantly.

The Watcher looked from me to Brian, who gave a slight nod. Richie shook his head and muttered "your funeral" as he moved to unlock the door.

Despite my confidence that Pete wouldn't hurt me, I still had to fight the instinct to flee as I stepped into the room with the large wolf. I paused at the door, not wanting to spook Pete when he was likely still disorientated.

I needn't have worried, however. Pete limped to my side and nudged me with his head, whining in a way made me want to wrap my arms around him and hug him tight.

"Are you okay?" I asked, crouching down so I could examine him for any sign of injury.

He nodded and opened his mouth but snapped it closed again. Another low whine rumbled from him, and he began to pace in clear agitation.

I couldn't help feeling like he wanted to tell me something, but he wouldn't be able to do that until we reunited him with his human body. The plan had been for his human body to remain at Teagan's apartment for safety reasons, so we needed to get back there ASAP.

As the thought occurred to me, another followed in its wake. Didn't it seem odd that all three of us had somehow ended up here at the Watchers HQ? It was a hell of a coincidence, given the timing. My own agitation rose to match Pete's, and I fought to keep it from showing.

"We should really get him back so he can rest properly. My car is still at Jessie's house."

Teagan moved to my side and gave the wolf's head a gentle rub. "My car is here. We can grab yours on the way back."

I waited a beat for the protest that I was sure would

come, but Brian simply stepped aside and let the three of us walk out of the small white room.

"If you need further assistance from any of our doctors, let me know," he said with a nod to Pete. Then he turned his focus to me. "I would very much like to talk more about our proposal once you've had time to consider it further. Richie will see you all out."

My wariness only grew as we made our way back up to ground level. I kept one hand on Pete's furred back the whole time and was relieved to see his limp was only mild. But the tension in his muscled form was unmistakable. Teagan, too, seemed on edge, though thankfully her eye colour stayed its natural shade. I didn't know what was causing the heightened tension, but something felt very wrong and I didn't like it.

When we reached the reception, my phone started to buzz insistently. I hurried to dig my phone out of my pocket, barely taking notice as Richie made his excuses and left.

Granny O'Meara's name flashed on the screen, and I frowned. She never called me. In fact, the only reason she even owned a phone was because we'd made her get one so we could check in on her.

"Granny?" I answered, the unease that had been plaguing me now doing a hula dance around my head.

"Ah, Aisling dear. Is your mother with you?"

"Mam?" My frown deepened. "No. I haven't seen her in a couple of weeks. What's wrong?"

"Oh, I'm sure it's nothing. She was meant to come visit me this afternoon, but she probably just forgot."

A chill of foreboding slithered through me. With everything going on, it wasn't too surprising I was on edge, but that didn't mean I needed to overreact now. I did my best to ignore the feeling and stay calm.

"Have you tried calling her? You know how mam can be. She's away with the fairies as the best of times."

"Oh no, I checked with the fairies and they haven't seen her either."

I blinked and shook my head. Though I'd seen the signs of the fairies that occupied my granny's garden, I highly doubted my mam had a clue about their existence, let alone that she'd have gotten waylaid visiting them.

"Let me see if I can get hold of her," I said, my voice distant to my ears as Pete's low growl echoed the pounding of my heart.

I promised to drop by for tea and biscuits soon and hung up. My hand was shaking as I moved to call my mam. I froze.

Three missed calls showed on the screen, followed by a single message. All from my mam.

Had we lost signal when we were underground?

I rushed to open the message, praying that there would be a simple explanation and that the alarm bells blaring in my head were unnecessary. The hope lasted for the entirety of a heartbeat. Then my blood turned to ice.

WE ASKED NICELY. NOW WE DO IT THE
HARD WAY.

CHAPTER SEVENTEEN

My fingers were trembling so much that it took me three tries to press the call button. The phone rang and rang, but my mam didn't answer. And neither did whoever sent that message.

Concern was written all over Teagan's face as she watched me silently. Pete paced next to us, the source of his agitation suddenly all too clear.

"We need to go to my mam's house," I said, a strange numbness settling over me as I hung up the phone.

Teagan gave a sharp nod and took me by the elbow. "We'll take my car. It'll be quicker than stopping to collect yours."

With a comforting efficiency, she led the way out of the building. I waited until the three of us had bundled into her car and were safely out of earshot before filling them in on my granny's call and the message from my mam's number. It was an effort to keep my voice from cracking as I brought them up to speed. The whole time, questions spun around my head, each getting more and more worrying.

Where was my mam?

Had the Order taken her?

What would they do to her if they had?

The drive to my mam's house was the longest of my life. I hit the redial button on my phone over and over, but to no avail. No matter how much I tried to convince myself that she'd simply lost track of time, the crippling twist of my gut told me otherwise.

I had the door open before Teagan had even pulled the car to a complete stop, and Pete was hot on my heels as I bolted to the front door of my mam's house. Fumbling in my pocket for my keys, I pounded on the door, all the while praying, "Please be home. Please be home. Please be home."

My hands were shaking so badly that when Teagan joined my side, she took the keys from me and unlocked the door. Pete pushed past us both, stalking into the house. I didn't wait to see if he gave the all-clear before following.

"Mam?" I called. Silence mocked me in return.

Oh god. Would we find her lying on the floor in one of the rooms? Would she be alive?

Swallowing back the bile that rose in my throat, I moved to the first door on my right, the living room. It was empty. No dead body, and no signs that anything had been disturbed.

Teagan stayed by my side as I headed for the

kitchen at the end of the hall. The door was slightly ajar and my palms were sweaty as I nudged it the rest of the way open. Sun shone through the large window, highlighting the dust motes that floated in the air. A stack of coffee cups were piled next to the sink waiting to be washed, but there was no other sign that anyone had been here recently. There was no half-eaten plate of food to indicate a meal interrupted, and no sign of my mam.

Before we could turn our attention to the upper level, Pete appeared on the stairs. He gave a shake of his head and a low whine. She wasn't up there either.

My heart clenched painfully even as a messed-up relief filled me. If she wasn't here, then I could keep believing she was alive. Even if the Order had taken her... Even if she might not be alive for much longer.

I dropped to the floor, a sob wrenching free from my throat. The full realisation of the situation hit me and I gasped for air, struggling to breathe as panic took hold.

They'd taken her. They'd taken my mam. This was all my fault. I didn't show up at the meeting, and they'd taken her to teach me a lesson.

Teagan crouched down next to me and wrapped her arms around me. Pete was at our side in a second, pressing against me, his solid warmth helping to ground me.

"What do we do?" I whispered, sucking in a shuddery breath.

Smoothing my hair back from my face, Teagan

looked at Pete. "Was there anything upstairs to suggest where they might have taken her? A note? Anything?"

Again, the large wolf shook his head.

The need to scream almost overwhelmed me and I buried my head in my hands. My mam was out there somewhere, with god only knew who doing god only knew what to her, and I had no clue how to help her.

Except...

I yanked my phone out of my pocket, a renewed sense of determination filling me. I scrolled to the one person who might actually have answers for me and hit the call button.

"Did you do this?" I demanded as soon as the call was answered.

"Aisling?" Bres's confusion was palpable even through the phone, but I refused to be distracted.

"Did you arrange this because I refused to help you?" I demanded again.

"Aisling, what the hell are you talking about? Calm down and tell me what's happened?"

"They've taken her." My voice cracked despite my best intentions. "They've taken my mam."

Silence filled the line for a heartbeat, and when Bres spoke again, his voice was hard, the restrained edge of anger in complete juxtaposition to the screaming inside my own head.

"The Order took her?"

I nodded even though he couldn't see me. Fear was choking me so much that I barely trusted myself to speak.

"Where are you?" he demanded.

Where she should be. Home. Safe.

I didn't say that, of course. Instead, I took a shuddery breath and straightened. If Bres hadn't been involved in this, then I needed only one thing from him.

"I need you to send me Bannon's number," I said, ignoring his question.

"What? No! Aisling, this is exactly what he wants. Let me at least look into it for you first."

"Please, Bres." The whispered words halted his refusal, and I pressed. "It's my mam. Surely you must understand."

His sharp inhale sent a jolt of guilt through me. Before I could apologise, he replied softly, "I'll send it. But please, let me check it out first. Don't do anything rash."

He hung up without waiting for an answer, and my phone buzzed a moment later with notice that a new contact had been shared with me.

Declan Bannon.

I took a moment to compose myself. I was under no illusions as to who held the power in this situation, but I'd be damned if I let Bannon hear me sniffling and begging. Teagan squeezed my shoulder and Pete pressed closer to me still, both trying to lend their strength in whatever way they could. When I hit the call button, there was no tremble to my hand.

"Ms. O'Meara," Bannon answered, satisfaction filling every bit of his smarmy self-assured tone. "It seems you can be resourceful when provided with the correct motivation."

"Where is she?" I demanded.

"Oh, she's perfectly safe. And she will remain that way so long as you co-operate with us like a good little Guardian."

My shoulders tensed and my grip tightened on the phone. "What do I have to do?"

"It's simple. Bring us the ritual in three days. Same place. Same time. Fail to show up this time, and there will be no more chances."

A chill ran through me as the line went dead.

Three days, same as before. Only this time I had no doubt that he would kill my mam if I didn't show. Unfortunately for both of us, there was zero guarantee that I could uncover the ritual in time.

CHAPTER EIGHTEEN

Bannon's ominous warning repeated over and over in my mind as we made our way back to Teagan's apartment. It killed me to just walk away from my mam's house with no further answers, but I was also antsy to get Pete back to his human body. With everything going on, it felt like tempting fate to keep him and his wolf separated for too long.

Once we were home and Pete was back to his normal self, the sense of helplessness struck me yet again. I slumped into the soft cushions of the sofa and dropped my head in my hands. "What do we do?"

Teagan sat down beside me and rubbed my back in soothing circles. "She's alive, Aisling. That's what you need to focus on right now."

I sniffled and nodded. She was right. I wouldn't be any use to my mam if I fell apart now.

A low growl came from Pete, his human eyes still amber as his wolf lurked close beneath the surface.

"This is my fault. I should've been watching your mam, not going off on some half-cocked quest."

I gave him a stern look, my misery temporarily forgotten. "No. This is not your fault, and I won't let you blame yourself. You got hit by a car, for god's sake."

He blew his unruly hair out of his face and frowned. "Yeah, I still don't know quite how that happened. I hadn't spotted any sign of the Order before..." He shook his head. "It doesn't matter. We need a plan."

"Well, we can't give them what we don't have," Teagan said. "So, we need to focus on how to get your mam away from the Order."

Which was great in theory, but the Order had shown us time and again that we were no match for them.

I sighed. "We're going to need help."

Pete's watchful eyes shone with understanding. "You're going to ask the Watchers."

A sickening nausea twisted inside me, but I nodded. "The Order have numbers on their side. We don't. Brian is a Garda. Surely he has to do something if I report a kidnapping to him."

"The Order won't have left any evidence," Teagan pointed out, far too logically for my liking. "If you report them to the police, you'll be accusing the party most likely to be our next head of government, and it will be your word against theirs."

I groaned. She was right. Brian and the Watchers would believe me, but there was no way I could go through normal channels with any of this. And something told me any help from the Watchers would come at a cost.

With that knowledge pressing heavily on me, I picked up my phone and rang Brian, putting it on speakerphone so everyone could hear.

He answered on the second ring. "Aisling. Is everything okay?"

My mouth was suddenly dry, and it took me two tries before I could form the words. "The Order took my mam. They're holding her ransom in exchange for the ritual."

The silence on the other end of the phone was deafening.

"What are your instructions?"

I filled him in on Bannon's orders, omitting the part about how I got Bannon's number in the first place. When I was finished, I was once more met with a long silence.

"We won't be able to do anything about this officially. We would have no way of explaining the Order's motivation."

Pete's low rumble was heavy with warning, and I shivered. "You can't seriously be turning your back on this."

"I'm not saying that," Brian hurried to reassure us. "But intervening in this situation would put my people in grave danger. I have to consider all the risks."

Desperation tightened like a steel band around my

chest, making it hard to breathe. He had to help. He just had to.

"You said you wanted us to work together." I let the words hang in the air, hoping he'd follow them to an implied conclusion.

He was quiet for a long moment before finally saying, "Let me gather a team. We'll agree on the best course of action, and I'll call you back."

I began to protest that we should be involved in any discussions, but the only response I got was a dial tone. Swearing at the phone, I hung up and flopped back into the cushions of the sofa. Teagan and Pete both watched me with concerned expressions.

"What will you do if they refuse to help?" Teagan asked, coming to sit next to me.

"They'll help. I all but told Brian his stupid Claiming idea was a no-go if they don't."

I was sure he wouldn't be happy with having his own words thrown back at him, but right now I didn't have the energy to care. If I had to agree to help the Watchers Claim magic in order to get my mam back safely, I'd do it. Considering I still didn't know what the ritual entailed, it would be an empty promise anyway.

More than an hour passed before Brian finally called back. By that time myself, Teagan, and Pete had considered and discarded more than twenty possible courses of action. Frustration was mounting for all of us. I felt like screaming.

I answered Brian's call and placed him on speaker-phone. "Tell me you have a plan."

"We believe our best option is to comply with the Order's demands."

I gaped at the phone dumbstruck. "You want me to deliver the ritual to them?"

"Of course not. We simply want them to think that. You will contact Bannon and confirm you're willing to make the trade, but demand to see your mother first. We'll have a team on standby, ready to come in as soon as they bring her out."

I didn't have to see Pete's frown to sense the displeasure rolling off him. "So, you're risking her mam's life on the off-chance that you can overpower them before they have a chance to harm her."

"We believe we have sufficient resources at our disposal to control the situation," Brian responded, seeming unfazed by the accusation. "Given our lack of information regarding Mrs. O'Meara's whereabouts, our options are limited."

"Ms," I corrected him numbly. My mam had never married and always got a bee in her bonnet when people made assumptions. The least I could do for her now was ensure she was being addressed properly.

"Ms. O'Meara," Brian acknowledged.

"What if they don't bring her to the trade?"

"Then you will refuse to hand over the ritual and demand that the trade is rescheduled until proof of life can be provided."

Proof of life. The room began to spin, and I had to fight the urge to vomit. What if she was already dead? What if they had killed her because of me?

Teagan reached out and squeezed my hand. I looked up into her determined blue eyes, and the panic that had threatened to drown me receded.

Blue eyes.

Teagan hadn't had any premonitions. Surely she'd have seen it if my mam was dead.

Letting that realisation ground me, I squared my shoulders and mentally prepared myself for what needed to be done. "Talk me through the plan step-by-step."

CHAPTER NINETEEN

The Watchers' plan was still sitting uneasily with me as night fell. I'd spent the evening casting furtive glances at Teagan's eyes for even a hint of purple, and I was sure she had to be completely freaked out. Still, that small bit of reassurance was the only thing that allowed me to finally close my eyes so that sleep could take me.

My longing to talk to Killian was stronger than any guilt I might feel at burdening him with yet more problems. I willed the dreamscape into existence even as I braced myself for what I would find.

The darkness receded but not fully. I blinked in confusion. It was night. The dreamscape had never been in night before. Shivering, I took in the eerie calm of the meadow and the moon overhead. The light of the moon made the dark cracks in the sky even more ominous, and I found myself staring at it like it was a ticking bomb counting down its final hours.

I climbed to my feet and followed the path through the woods to Killian's house. When I got there, however, the door was open but the house was empty. Refusing to give in to the worry that tightened my chest, I continued around the back of the stone building.

A narrow trail led further downhill and as I followed it, I heard the burbling of running water in the distance. I caught sight of Killian a moment later. He was sitting by a small stream with his back to me, and two strange shapes hung in the air in front of him.

I slowed my footsteps as I grew closer, and the shapes became clearer. My breath hitched.

Dub and Carmen hung motionless in the air above the stream. Their bodies had a strangely translucent quality to them, and somehow I knew I wasn't actually looking at their physical forms. This was a representation of the subconsciousnesses that Killian was holding trapped here.

"The water helps to hold their magic at bay," Killian said, not turning to look at me as I came to a stop at his side. "It's easier to breathe here."

I lowered myself to the ground next to him and took in his profile. The dark circles under his eyes were more pronounced, the skin tight with tension, but he seemed more lucid than the last few times I'd seen him.

"What will happen to them when the dreamscape goes? Will they wake up?"

He shook his head. "Their conscious minds will fade with the dreamscape. Everything here will."

A sharp pain shot through my chest. *Everything here will.* Everything – including him.

I swallowed hard, not knowing what to say. I wasn't ready to admit defeat as far as he was concerned. Not until I'd exhausted all options.

My mind jumped back to the note in my ancestor's book about energy. The book had said it couldn't be destroyed, only changed. If that was the case… "What will happen to their magic? Will it die with them?"

Killian's jaw tightened. "No. It will have to return eventually."

I frowned. "I don't understand. You've been draining yourself to hold it back. Why would you do that if it's going to return anyway?" Accusation caused my voice to rise higher. He could have prolonged the deterioration. We could have had more time to help him. Why would he put himself through all of this if it was going to make no difference in the end?

He turned to me finally and there was a softness in his dark eyes that cracked my heart wide open. He reached out and cupped my cheek, running a rough thumb over it.

"To buy you time. Dub and Carmen's magic is powerful. If it returns and the wrong people find a way to access it… You're strong, Aisling. Stronger than you know. But you have a hard road ahead of you, and if there's anything I can do to ease the burden of what's to come, I'll do it."

My throat tightened and I looked away. I didn't want him to see my fear. He was placing so much faith in me, and I was so far out of my depth that I couldn't see the shore anymore. He let his hand drop and allowed me the privacy to gather my thoughts.

"Why did you agree to this?" I asked softly. "You gave up your life to be held in stasis, only to exist here for a finite amount of time before finally dying."

"Many of our people gave up their lives."

I shook my head. "That's different. I'm not saying their sacrifice wasn't noble, but there was an end for them. If I hadn't been stupid enough to release the magic, you'd have been stuck in limbo forever."

"I'd have deserved it."

He said the words so quietly that I almost thought I'd imagined them, but I didn't imagine the loathing that was thick in his tone or the way he cast his eyes down in shame.

I put a hand on his arm and searched his face. "Talk to me, Killian."

He closed his eyes and breathed deeply through his nose. When he opened his eyes again he was staring across the stream, but I could tell his mind was somewhere far away.

"It was my fault. When the head Council of the Tuatha put forward the idea of the sacrifice, I was against it. I'd been married to Maedbh for less than a year, and we'd just found out she was expecting our first child. I had everything to live for and I didn't want to give that up, not even to protect the magic.

"I worked in secret with Maedbh and her family to find another way to stop the Fomorians. She came from a long line of powerful magic users, a line that would ultimately be the origin of the Guardian. We found a way to hide the Claiming ritual in a book so that only those of Maedbh's bloodline could access it."

He turned to me, smiling slightly as my eyes widened. "Yes, Aisling, in your book. We thought it would fix everything. The Fomorians couldn't Claim the magic without the necessary ritual, and the window of opportunity would soon pass. But we were betrayed. My cousin learned of what we had done and told the Fomorians."

This time there was no concealing my shock. "Why would he do that?" I asked, horrified at the thought of Killian's own family betraying him like that.

"My cousin hated the Fomorians, but he hated the Tuatha also. He was a product of both and wanted by neither. I later found out that he was helping the Fomorians so he could use their avarice against us all when the barriers were at their weakest."

"He wanted to destroy the magic," I whispered, understanding dawning. It was Bres's ancestor he was talking about, Bres's ancestor who had betrayed them.

Killian nodded, his expression becoming closed as he carefully locked down the emotions that were no doubt rearing their head with the memories.

"So, the Fomorians learned of the book and how to access the ritual. One day when I was at yet another Council meeting, pleading my case for them to stay their hand, the Fomorians sent men to my home. They threatened the life of our unborn child to make Maedbh give up the ritual. Then they killed her anyway. I came home to find my wife dead and our unborn child cut from her body."

A sob lodged in my throat and I covered my mouth, shaking my head as if that might change the truth of what he was saying. His wife. His child. Oh god, I hadn't known. I hadn't even come close to imagining the true extent of what drove him.

"Once the Fomorians had the ritual and Maedbh was gone," Killian went on tonelessly, "there was no reason to fight the Council's plans anymore. They needed a dreamwalker, and I needed to atone for my failure. I wasn't there for her when she needed me, but I wouldn't fail her again."

"So, you signed yourself up for a lifetime of purgatory?" I took both his hands in mine and forced him to face me. "Killian, it's not your fault your wife died. She wouldn't have wanted this for you."

"No, she wouldn't. But at least now when I finally get to see her again, I know I can look her in the eyes and tell her that I made it right." He smiled sadly, his eyes roaming my face. "You remind me of her, you know. You have her strength."

I cast my eyes away, reminded yet again of just how weak and helpless I felt right now. "They have my mam," I said quietly.

Killian's grip tightened on mine. "What?" he demanded.

"The Order. They took my mam, and they're holding her as leverage to force me to bring them the ritual."

He stood and shoved a hand through his hair, anger turning his eyes stormy. "Of course they are. When are they expecting you to hand it over?"

"Three days." I looked up at the night sky. "Well, two now I guess. Not that I have a clue how to find the ritual anyway."

Killian paced back and forth, the muscle in his jaw jumping as he clenched his hair by the roots. He looked at the two forms hovering over the stream and up at the moon shining above. Then he turned to face.

"I do."

CHAPTER TWENTY

I was reeling as the dreamscape faded, leaving me alone once more with the cold light of morning and my own thoughts. Killian had given me the answer I needed to save my mam. The answer that could doom us all. He had trusted me with the key to finding the Claiming ritual and told me he had faith in me to do the right thing.

I didn't know what the right thing was, dammit. And I had less than two days to figure it out.

Needing to burn off some of the frustration that clouded my head like a black fog, I shoved the covers off me and climbed out of bed. The fact it took me more than five minutes to find my running gear probably said a lot about how well I was keeping up with my health and fitness, but there was no time to start like the present, right?

Careful not to wake Pete, who had taken up residence on Teagan's sofa, I crept out of the apartment and made my way down to the ground floor. My steps skidded to a halt, however, when I spotted Bres hovering outside the gates of the apartment block. He looked uncharacteristically unsure of himself as he stared at the panel of buzzers that rang through to each of the individual apartments.

I debated heading back upstairs. I could pretend I hadn't seen him and simply ignore it if he chose to press the buzzer for Teagan's apartment.

Or, I could be an adult.

With a weary sigh, I huddled into my running jacket and made my way out to the gate. Bres looked up at my approach, the uncertainty even more pronounced on his features as he searched my face.

"What are you doing here?" I wrapped my arms around myself as much to contain the mess of emotions rearing inside me as from the sharp bite of the morning air.

"I was debating with myself what would be an acceptable time to call."

"And what did you decide?"

"I was hoping you might forgive the early visit given I have information you're going to want to hear."

I raised an eyebrow and waited.

"I know where your mam is."

My heart stopped beating for so long that I numbly wondered if I'd had a heart attack and not realised it. Hope surged in me and I viciously shoved it back down, clenching my fists as if that alone could protect me.

"If you know where she is," I said slowly, carefully, "why didn't you say so when I called yesterday?" Yesterday – when I outright accused him of playing a part in my mam's kidnapping.

"I didn't know for sure. I wanted to check it out myself before I said anything."

"You wanted to check it out..." Realisation cut me like a knife as I took in the shadows that haunted his eyes. "You didn't want me to be the one to find her if they'd already killed her," I whispered.

He looked away, but not before I caught the tight line of his lips or how he closed his eyes as if in pain. It was an effort to form my next words.

"Is she –"

"She's alive." His head snapped back around as he hurried to reassure me. "From what I could see, she's being well looked after."

I swallowed hard against the burning in my throat. It was an effort not to crumble to the ground in over-whelming relief, but I needed to hold myself together. Safe now didn't guarantee safe in the future.

"I thought you didn't know where the Order were."

"I didn't. At least not until recently. Part of the reason I went to the charity event the other night was to see if I could place some trackers on the Order's cars. It didn't sit comfortably with me not knowing where they are."

The explanation made sense. And right now, my head was too much of a mess to worry about whether or not he was telling the truth – so long as he was right about my mam being alive. I needed to think, and I needed to clear my head to do that.

"Did you happen to spot any coffee shops that were open on your way here?"

He nodded and I let him lead me in silence to a small place about ten minutes from Teagan's apartment.

The cafe was quiet, aside from the odd person popping in to grab coffee on the way to the office. When Bres stepped up to the counter, the woman's smile brightened so much I almost had to shield my eyes.

"Hot chocolate?" he asked, looking at me.

"Make it a triple shot latte with extra caramel syrup." My nervous system was unlikely to thank me for it, but I needed my wits about me for this conversation.

We waited – me not so patiently – for our drinks before making our way to a table at the back of cafe. I took a drink of my latte, wincing at the bitterness beneath the copious amounts of syrup, and gave Bres all of two seconds to sit down before demanding, "Where is she?

"A house on the far side of the city. It's the house I grew up in before my..." He shook his head and took a drink of his own coffee. "Unless things have changed, the Order own all the properties on the street. From the outside it's just a well-off residential estate, but it's regularly patrolled and security is high."

Disappointment caused the caffeine to churn in my

empty stomach, and I pushed the mug away from me. What had I expected, that the Order would be holding her somewhere I could just waltz into?

"And you actually saw her?" *Please say you saw her. Please say you know for a fact she's alive.*

"With my own two eyes."

Some of the tension I'd been holding eased at his confirmation. I cast my eyes down as tears burned my eyes and threatened to spill over.

"What are you going to do?" Bres asked, the gentle understanding in his tone more than I could deal with right now.

I squared my shoulders and lifted my head; feeling sorry for myself would do nothing to help my mam. "The Watchers want me to play along with Bannon's demands. They think I should stage the trade and they'll swoop in and grab my mam."

"The Watchers? Have you lost your mind? What were you thinking getting them involved? You can't trust them, Aisling."

It was an effort not to let my surprise at his outburst show on my face. He'd never kept his opinion of the Watchers secret, but there was genuine concern widening his eyes. He needn't have worried, however. I'd already decided to listen to my gut on this one – their plan sucked. I wouldn't have been so quick to share the details with him otherwise.

"I was thinking that the Order have my mam and I've no chance of facing them on my own. What would you suggest, Bres?"

He drummed his fingers on the table, clearly struggling to rein in his agitation. "Bannon isn't going to bring your mam to the trade-off. He'll tell you what you want to hear to ensure he gets the ritual, but we both know he's not going to give up his leverage over you until the Claiming is complete."

"I know."

His brow furrowed in confusion. "Then why are going along with their ridiculous suggestion?"

"I'm not."

His hand stilled as his expression became shuttered. "You don't want me to know what you're really planning because you don't trust me."

"Do you blame me?"

"No. But believe me when I say this, Aisling, I have no intention of letting the Order take anybody else's mother from them."

My heart gave an odd flutter at his fierce declaration. I looked away, not wanting him to see the confusion on my face. Killian's words from the night before were still fresh in my mind, as was the warning he had given me previously about Bres's intentions. I'd be a fool to trust him. He even said so himself. So, why did I find myself wanting so badly to believe he meant what he said?

"What side did your ancestors take?" I asked. "I know you were raised by the Order, but your bloodline straddles both sides of this fight. Which side did they take when the Tuatha made the choice to sacrifice themselves?"

This time it was Bres's turn to look away. "The wrong one," he said softly.

Wrong, as in they sided with the Fomorians? Wrong, as in his ancestor played a deadly game of chess in a bid to destroy magic, only to ultimately lose?

I couldn't tell from his answer how much Bres truly knew, but I decided it didn't matter. One way or the other, I was going to save my mam. The only question was what I'd have to sacrifice to do it.

"Take me to where they're holding my mam," I said finally. "I need to see her for myself."

CHAPTER TWENTY-ONE

"This is a bad idea," Bres muttered, shifting his weight as he crouched down next to me behind the greenest hedge I'd ever seen.

I ignored him as I kept my gaze fixed on the large white detached house situated at the centre of a manicured lawn on the far side of our hiding place. He'd been arguing the same point ever since I'd insisted on seeing for myself where my mam was being held. Given the thrum of magic that stole my breath as soon as we neared the estate, I couldn't disagree with his assessment that it was dangerous for us to be here. But I didn't care. I needed to see for myself that my mam was okay, and I needed to figure out how the hell to get her out of here.

In the few minutes that we'd been here, I'd already caught sight of the security patrolling the grounds, and indeed the entire estate. Large gates acted as a deterrent to anyone looking to approach the house. But if what Bres said was true, neither of those were our biggest problem.

"Show me where the boundaries of the ward are."

"Aisling –"

I quieted him with a glare.

He sighed. "Fine. But all you do is look. I mean it, Aisling. This ward will turn you to ash if you even come within breathing distance of it."

Though it wasn't the first time he'd warned me as much, a shiver of unease still set my nerves on edge. It seemed the Order hadn't wasted much time in updating their security measures since the return of magic. I was just hoping that they hadn't counted on someone being able to siphon the power from their fancy ward – assuming I was able to, of course.

Keeping low, we crept along the hedge line towards the left-hand corner of the house. I spotted the unusual looking stone placed there before Bres stopped to point it out to me. I didn't recognise the symbols carved into the stone, but there was no mistaking the energy that radiated from it.

I chewed my lip, considering my options.

"How many of these are there around the house?"

"Seven."

Just like the standing stones at the Church of the Blessed Heart. People might say that seven is a lucky number, but I was beginning to hate it.

"And what happens if one of them is moved out of place?"

"Uh-uh." He shook his head and crossed his arms

as he fixed me with a stern look. "To move them, you'd have to touch them. You touch them, you die."

"But what about –" I snapped my mouth shut as the sound of voices came from within the grounds of the house.

Bres pulled me around the corner of the hedge and held his finger to his lips as he bent low.

My heart tap-danced in my chest as I crouched next to him and turned my attention to the gates where a security guard had just appeared. Bill stood at his side, gripping his arm tightly, though showing no other sign of aggression.

"Changing of the guard," Bres whispered in my ear, his breath causing me to shiver for entirely different reasons. "They need someone tied to the wards to help them get through safely."

They didn't even trust their own men to come and go? Shit. Maybe it wasn't going to be as easy as I hoped to get through.

Not that it was going to stop me from trying.

"I want to see my mam."

The displeasure was clear on Bres's face, but he knew by now that he was wasting his time arguing. Jaw clenched, he gave a wary look to the front gates where Bill was still facilitating the changeover of the security rotation. He turned with a silent nod, beckoning me on towards the rear of the property.

I followed along the line of the hedge, my gaze scanning the ground for any more of the ward stones as we moved. Would I be better off trying to siphon the ward's magic at the anchor points, or would it be weaker at the gaps between? Since my experience with wards was limited to, well, this one, it was probably going to be a case of follow my gut and hope for the best.

Two more ward stones later, and we came to a stop at the rear of the property. From the back, it looked like any other family home. Security was nowhere to be seen here, but I had no doubt they were close by and ready to act should we, by some miracle, make it past the ward.

Bres pointed to a window on the second floor. "That's where I spotted her last time. Unless the layout has changed since I was a boy, it's a double bedroom with en-suite."

I gritted my teeth. Nice to know they were keeping her in comfort, but the civility of it all was nearly more sickening than them showing their true colours. Did Bannon have someone bringing her room service? Had he managed to convince her that they were keeping her there for her own safety? It seemed like the kind of messed-up head game he'd enjoy playing.

Every muscle in my body was tense as I watched the window for even a hint of movement. Time seemed to stop and only the burning in my chest told me that I was holding my breath.

Then it happened. A figure moved into view at the edge of the window. She turned in profile, and I caught my first proper glimpse of her. My mam.

Without thinking, I launched up off the ground.

The hedge might have been a solid wall for all it stood between me and my mam, but I shoved at it, determined to get through to the other side.

Bres grabbed my arm and yanked me back so forcefully that I fell on my arse. "What the hell do you think you're doing?"

My retort died on the tip of my tongue as my phone began to buzz insistently in my pocket. I pulled it out to see Pete's name flashing on the screen.

I didn't even get a chance to speak as Pete's panicked voice cut in as soon as I answered the phone. "Aisling, whatever you're doing, you need to stop. Right now."

"Pete, calm down," I whispered, covering my mouth with my hand to muffle the sound as much as I could. "What's wrong?"

"Teagan. Her eyes went all funny, and she keeps zoning in and out. She's just saying your name over and over."

"Shit." I looked at the hedge, and the ward that I knew lay beyond it.

Okay, so maybe I hadn't quite been thinking clearly when I tried to barge through it. But that didn't mean I couldn't siphon –

"Wherever you are, you need to get out of there. Don't make your best friend see your death, Aisling."

His words washed over me like ice water. Of course I didn't want that for Teagan. Hell, I didn't want to die either. But the thought of leaving my mam here was almost too much to bear.

"Okay," I said quietly, my heart dropping. "Tell Teagan it's okay. I'll be home soon."

I ended the call and hung my head. "We have to leave her here, don't we?"

Bres reached over and took my hand in his. "I'm sorry, Aisling. I tried to warn you. But trust me, I'll do everything I can to help you find a way. A way that doesn't put you both in danger."

Because the Order would have no problem killing my mam if I gave them cause to.

Bres was right; there was no option here where I could hope to waltz in there and safely take her with me. If I was being honest with myself, there was probably no way I could get in there full stop without their agreement – not if Teagan's warning vision was anything to go by. Which left me with very few options.

"I think we should probably go." I let go of Bres's hand and turned away, not wanting him to see the pain on my face.

He placed the hand on the small of my back and led me back the way we'd come. We reached the front corner of the house when he froze.

I followed his line of sight, then hissed in a breath when I spotted Bill standing barely ten feet away from us on the far side of the hedge. He had his head cocked to the side and his shrewd eyes were scanning the perimeter of the house. If I didn't know better, I'd swear he knew we were there.

Though I had no idea what, if any, magic the Order's museum curator had, the tension radiating from Bres told me everything I needed to know. When he urged me forward, I obeyed without argument.

I made it almost to the edge of the perimeter when my foot landed on a branch on the ground. The snap of wood might as well have been a gunshot as it echoed in the silence.

Through the hedge, I saw Bill's head whip around in our direction. A slow smile spread across his face, chilling me to my very core.

"Run," Bres urged in a frantic whisper. "I'll lead him away. Get as far away from here as you can."

He didn't give me a chance to argue. He just turned and sprinted in the opposite direction, making no effort to stay quiet.

I hesitated, not wanting to leave until I knew he had enough of a head start to get away safely. But given that was counter-productive to his plan, I cast a final look towards Bill, who had taken the bait and was now striding in the direction Bres had gone. Then despite my better judgement, I moved as quickly and as quietly as I could away from the house. Leaving my mam and Bres behind.

CHAPTER TWENTY-TWO

I waited until I was as far away as possible before calling Bres. His phone rang out, so I hung up, deciding it best not to call again in case I gave his position away if Bill was still nearby. Resigned to making my own way home, I called Pete instead and asked him and Teagan to come pick me up.

Guilt gnawed at me for leaving Bres behind, but when Pete assured me that Teagan's visions had died down as soon as I'd made myself scarce, I took that as a positive sign. Besides, Bres was a master of getting out of sticky situations; he didn't need me worrying about him.

As soon as I climbed into the back seat of Pete's car, I leaned forward between the front seats. "What exactly did you see?" I asked, taking in the tightness that remained in Teagan's expression, despite the natural blue of her eyes.

She shook her head. "It wasn't clear. I could see a shimmering barrier, and I just knew that whatever decision you made in relation to it would determine the outcome."

Shimmering barrier? The ward, presumably.

I gave an involuntary shiver and sat back in the seat, buckling myself in as Pete pulled out into traffic. That had been reckless of me. If I didn't learn to think clearly through heightened emotion, I was going to get more than just myself killed. I needed to be smarter.

Pete glanced back at me in the rear-view mirror. "Care to fill us in on what you were up to?"

I did, starting from Bres's appearance that morning to seeing my mam in the flesh for that brief, reassuring glimpse.

"Maybe the Watchers can find a way onto the property?" Pete suggested once I'd finished.

"No!"

Teagan's response took us both by surprise.

She shook her head. "I don't think that warning vision was limited to Aisling. Whatever that shimmering barrier was, it felt like death."

I grimaced. "So, staging a rescue is probably out of the question while they're holding her there. Which means we need a different plan."

"I take it that means the Watchers' plan is off the table?" Pete said, no surprise in his voice – we'd all known the plan was terrible.

Teagan twisted in her seat to look back at me. "What are you thinking?"

I hesitated, wondering if I was making yet another mistake, but not too sure what else to do.

"Killian told me how to find the ritual. I think we need to understand exactly what is involved in it if we've any chance of stopping it. I won't let the Order have access to that much power, but I can't let them hurt my mam either. We need to find another way."

There was no argument from either of my friends. Pete simply asked, "What do you need?"

It took twenty minutes for us to head back to Teagan's apartment so I could fetch my ancestor's book and our sharpest kitchen knife. Then we were on the road again. The drive to the Church of the Blessed Heart was a textbook study in déjà vu, and the three of us were silent the entire way. It was only when Pete pulled to a stop in a lay-by on the narrow country road that I realised I was gripping the book in my lap so hard that my knuckles were white.

Teagan turned to me once more, forehead creased in concern. "You sure you want to do this?"

No. "Yes."

As risky as it was for us to uncover the details of the ritual, I couldn't keep operating blind. Sure, I had no doubt the Order were more than capable of torturing the details out of me, but they'd already shown the lengths they were willing to go to. That wouldn't change, whether or not I had the ritual. If anything, they'd only intensify their efforts to convince me to find it.

Together, we climbed out of the car and headed for

the entrance of the church grounds. As we approached the two large oak trees that formed an arch leading into the old graveyard, I was shocked to see signs of new life creeping along the blackened bark and bare branches. Carmen's magic had all but desecrated the land here in an effort to lure me out. Though the glimpses of brown and green were still few and far between, they gave me a surge of hope. Nature was fighting back against the darkness. Maybe we could too.

Similar signs of life could be seen as we made our way along the gravel path and into the graveyard. Patches of green were growing once more among the crumbling graves, and as I inhaled deeply, the quiet sound of birds chirping reached my ears. An odd sense of peace settled over me.

One of the few benefits of the damage wrought by Carmen was that there were no tourists milling about the area, so we didn't have to worry about prying eyes. I spared a quick glance towards my ancestor Betty Anne's destroyed grave beneath the still-withered cherry blossom tree and said a silent prayer asking her to guide me. Then with my head held high, I headed for the looming ruins of the church and the low stone wall beyond.

Every memory I had of this place flashed through my mind as we stepped over the low boundary wall and into the perfect green field on the other side. Though my eyes still told me the field before me was empty, every other sense I possessed now recognised the magic that surrounded me. I allowed it to wrap around me and give me the strength I'd need for what was to come.

I slowed my steps, turning to Teagan and Pete. "Keep watch. If you get even a hint that someone is coming, give the signal and then get the hell out of here."

Their silence told me in no uncertain terms what the chances were of them leaving me, but I didn't want to waste time arguing. I gave them both a quick hug and crossed the boundary of the illusion spell.

Seven large standing stones appeared before me, and I walked into the centre of the circle. I lowered myself to the ground and placed the book down in front of me. A calm silence blanketed the space, but my head was filled with the ghosts of those who came before, those who'd sacrificed themselves to protect us all.

If I did this, I was putting everything they'd done at risk. If I didn't... Well, that was a future I couldn't face.

So, with a trembling hand, I took hold of the kitchen knife I'd brought and ran the blade down the inside of my left arm. Blood welled up along the wound and slowly ran down the edge of my arm to drip onto the book.

The pages began flicking rapidly and a fierce wind rose up around me. I gritted my teeth in an effort to hold my position against the force of it, closing my eyes as my hair whipped into my face.

Then just as swiftly as it started, it was over.

I blinked and swiped away the tears that had filled my eyes from the wind's onslaught. Heavy mist surrounded me, so much so that the standing stones were barely visible. A glance down showed me that the book had come to rest open on pages that were blank. Disappointment coursed through me.

Had I done something wrong?

The instructions Killian had given me were simple. So, why hadn't it worked?

When I looked up again, a figure was walking towards me through the mist. I rose to my feet, body tense as I waited to see whether it was friend or foe.

I recognised the flowing strawberry blonde hair and green silk dress before the woman's features became visible through the mist's shroud. When they did, I was struck by the love shining in her eyes.

"You have made your decision, then?"

Her question floated on the wind as she came to a stop before me. I shook my head, my brow creasing as I tried to get a handle on my muddled thoughts.

"No. Yes. I mean, I need answers so I can find a way to save my mam. The Order took her."

The woman's smile turned sad and she reached out to caress my cheek. "We often have to make difficult decisions to save the ones we love."

"Did you?" I suddenly realised that I didn't even know the woman's name. Was she one of my ancestors? Was she the one who had written the letter in my book?

"Yes. And I would make them again. But only you can decide what you are willing to sacrifice for those you love."

"What if I make the wrong choice?" I whispered.

"Your heart will always see you true."

I snorted. "My heart is what got us into this mess."

She laughed and the sound was like music, free and joyous. "What is a heart for, if not to challenge us to become who we need to be? Make no mistake, my child, the world will place many obstacles in your path. But you have the blood of powerful women running through your veins. You simply need to believe in your own strength."

"Do I have your blood running through my veins?"

"No, my child. I'm not of your line. My blood runs in another. Like you, I simply wish to protect those I love, but you alone as the Guardian can make the next choice. I wish I could ease that burden for you, or make the path ahead easier. But I fear that is your cross to bear."

Lucky me.

I closed my eyes and pictured my mam's face. I pictured Teagan and Pete standing by my side as we faced almost-certain death at the hands of Dub and Carmen. I remembered the unyielding fate that filled every minute of Killian's teachings. And I even thought of Bres. Of the brief moments of vulnerability I'd witnessed, of the boy who'd been forced to grow up much too young, and of the man who still held a spark of goodness within him, even if he didn't yet know it himself.

With a shuddery breath, I opened my eyes. "Tell me what I need to do to reveal the ritual."

CHAPTER TWENTY-THREE

As it turned out, I only had to ask in order to learn the secret to the Claiming.

With my question, the wind whipped into a frenzy once more. I was forced to shield my face from the force of it, and when it finally ceased, I was once more standing alone at the centre of the stone circle, and I just *knew*.

My legs were wobbling worse than jelly as I stumbled back through the illusion boundary to collapse on my arse. Teagan and Pete were at my side in an instant.

"Are you hurt?"

"Dammit, we have to stop the blood."

I waved their concerns away weakly, but didn't protest when Teagan pulled out the small first aid kit we'd brought and started cleaning the cut on my arm.

"I'm okay. Things just got a little trippy there for a minute."

"Did you get what you needed?" There was an odd

glow to Teagan's eyes as she asked the question, and I swallowed hard.

"I got it. Let's get home first and I'll fill you both in – preferably with wine."

There were no arguments to that suggestion. We gathered our stuff and were back on the road in less than five minutes. As the wheels sped over the asphalt, my thoughts raged. Details of the Claiming ran through my mind, but the one thing that repeated itself over and over was the timeline. I'd known we were running out of time. I just hadn't realised how quickly.

Back at Teagan's, we settled ourselves in the living room, Teagan with her legs tucked up on the sofa next to me, and Pete leaning against the wall. We each held a full wine glass in hand, and there was another bottle ready to go when we needed it. The thought of drinking myself into oblivion was appealing, but likely to prove unproductive given my hangover recovery rate.

"You were right about the triple eclipse," I told Teagan, hugging my wine glass to me. "The first eclipse is the catalyst and the ritual causes time to fold in on itself, temporarily bringing the three eclipses in line to thin the veil."

"The first eclipse?" Teagan's eyes widened. "That's in..."

I nodded. "Four days."

"Well, shit."

Pete started pacing as agitation finally won out over

his calm veneer. It had taken less time than I expected, though I guess I had just informed them we were well and truly screwed.

"The ritual involves power, some key artefacts, and a trial to judge the person worthy of Claiming."

"What kind of trial?" Pete asked, frowning.

I shrugged. "That part wasn't too clear. But I got the feeling that it wouldn't be a simple maths test."

"And what happens if the trial isn't passed?"

I grimaced. "Also probably a case where ignorance is bliss."

"Do the Order have everything they need to complete the ritual?"

"I think so. They have the cauldron, and a fair amount of power inside it. The sword is one of the artefacts, though we'd already guessed that they didn't give it to me out of the goodness of their heart. The other two items are a spear from some guy named Lugh, and a piece of some magical stone thingy. I'm pretty sure I saw both of those in the case where Bannon originally kept the sword."

Teagan gave an amused snort at my less than reverent descriptions of what I could only assume were important historical artefacts.

"What's to stop them from completing the ritual themselves?" Pete asked, his footsteps slowing as he considered everything I'd shared so far.

"The magic hasn't fully returned yet. They need me to siphon the last of it from the dreamscape before it can be Claimed. And if I had to guess, I'd say Bannon knows there'll be a test of some sort and isn't too confident on passing it himself."

I took a gulp of my wine before placing the glass down on the floor next to me. "The ritual the Tuatha used to create the Guardian line was a variant of the Claiming ritual. It linked the ancestral line to the magic, which means I can act as a conduit within the main ritual and, I guess, direct the magic."

"What do you mean direct?" Teagan asked.

"Apparently, there's a narrow window of time once the trial is passed where the magic is untethered. During that time, I have to Claim it or choose to transfer it to another person or thing."

"Which is what Bannon is counting on," she finished, joining the dots to the logical conclusion.

"I would guess so, yeah."

"And presumably he'll continue to hold your mam hostage to ensure you go with door number two."

Silence fell in the room. I reached for my glass again, more as a distraction from the panic threatening to rise once more inside me than out of a need for a drink.

"What are we going to do?" Pete asked, coming to a complete stop in front of where Teagan and I sat.

I gave a small smile, grateful despite the circumstances for the two friends here by my side. "Something in the wording of the instructions gave me an idea, but it's risky." I gave Teagan a hopeful glance. "Any chance it was just low blood sugar levels messing with your visions earlier?"

She shook her head, apologetic. "The details weren't the clearest, but the warning was unmistakable. Any action that brought you closer to that house would have resulted in your death."

Unless I was escorted in...

"Okay. Then I need to speak to Killian. This affects him every bit as much as it does me, and I won't move forward without his agreement."

Pete raised an eyebrow, and I could have sworn I caught a flash of amber in his brown eyes. "Care to fill us in?"

"Soon. I promise."

I found Killian sitting at the same stream as before, only this time the dreamscape was in daylight once more. The two semi-transparent figures hung in the air before him, and a strange mass of black shadows writhed in the air between his hands.

"Is that their magic?" I asked, coming to sit on the ground beside him.

He didn't take his eyes from it as he nodded. "I found a way to condense the energy into a smaller space. It won't last for long, but it makes it easier for me to hold it here."

I stared into the swirling darkness, surprised to find that it didn't fill me with the sense of terror I normally associated with Dub and Carmen's power. If anything, the movements within the mass were almost elegant, beautiful to behold.

"Is that why it seems a bit more stable around here?" I gestured to the sky where the sun had once more made an appearance, even if the jagged cracks still scarred the clear blue.

Killian was quiet for a long moment, and the silent hope that had sparked inside me when the dreamscape first appeared withered and died.

"The calm always comes before the storm," he said softly, taking a split second to glance sideways at me. "Make no mistake, Aisling, the storm is coming."

I hugged my knees to me. There was no point in stamping my feet at the unfairness of it all, but damn if I didn't want to anyway. Instead, I looked around at the world that Killian had called home for longer than I could imagine. "Is there a way to stop it fading?"

"No. It is how it was always meant to be."

"Would you want me to try if there was?"

"No."

I nodded. Deep down, I'd known that would be his answer. He'd already told me that he was ready to see his wife again. But the grief that welled up inside me didn't want to listen to logic. It wanted the rail against the hand he'd been dealt.

"I've seen where the Order are holding my mam. She's alive, but they have a ward surrounding the property and when I debated crossing it, it triggered a warning vision for Teagan."

Killian snapped his head around, the black mass

spreading as his attention on it faltered. "You can't mess with the ward. If Teagan's powers flared up, you can guarantee it will be lethal."

I arched an eyebrow and looked pointedly at the darkness that was taking full advantage of his lapse in concentration to reach out its inky tendrils.

"We already figured that out," I said, once he had regained control again. "Which leaves us very few options."

"You accessed the ritual."

There was no censure – or worse, disappointment – is his tone, but still I hesitated before admitting, "Yes. It seemed like the only way we can make an informed decision."

"And what have you decided?"

"To hand in my resignation as Guardian?"

A smile tugged at the corner of his mouth, and once more my heart gave that damned twinge of pain. I wanted nothing more than for him to be happy. Even though I'd only known him a short time, it seemed strange to think he'd be gone soon. How was that fair?

He didn't push as I worked through my messed-up thoughts, simply stayed at my side as the same comforting presence he'd been from the start of this mess. In saying that he didn't want me to save the dreamscape, he'd all but given his blessing for the idea that had been forming in my mind since I stepped out of the stone circle. I needed to be sure it would work, though. Otherwise, I'd be damning us all.

"If I have things correct, I either need to Claim the

magic or bind it to another, otherwise it destroys me and returns to our world untethered and highly volatile?"

"In simple terms, yes."

"Can it be bound to anything?"

"It can be bound to anything with ... a degree of sentience. Magic doesn't mix well with manmade objects, but something natural, something that has evolved from the same energy source as the magic itself, could be used."

"And if I bound it to something that met that criteria, would a person then be able to access it and corrupt it for their own means?"

"There are always ways if someone wants something enough. But once the magic becomes an innate part of a thing, it is not easily separated."

"So, it's no less safe than if it was bound to a person?"

This time Killian did smile, but it was a sad smile, filled with the knowledge of many years of pain. "You could argue that it's safer, given it is people who corrupt magic to ill will and not the other way around."

CHAPTER TWENTY-FOUR

I tried not to let my nerves show as I lowered myself into one of the black leather chairs that surrounded the meeting room table at the Watchers HQ. Teagan took the chair to my right, and Pete the one to my left. Brian, for once, seemed happy enough to talk to us without any of the other Watchers present. I wondered if he'd come to regret that, though it likely made the conversation we were about to have easier.

"I understand you're concerned about your mam, Aisling, but I can assure you we –"

"That's not why we're here," I cut him off. "Well, not entirely."

He gave me the kind of patient look one might reserve for an unreasonable child and waited for me to continue. I sighed inwardly. *Play the game, Aisling. That's the only way this is going to work.*

"I've found the ritual."

Brian straightened, his attention sharpening so

quickly it was almost comical to watch. "Where did you find it?"

"In a book left to me by my ancestors. It was hidden by magic, set to only reveal itself to the Guardian." I carefully avoided mentioning that my blood was the key to accessing it. The Watchers might believe themselves to be the good guys, but I had no doubt they'd cross the line to torture if they believed it to be for the greater good.

I let the silence stretch out for a few moments, waiting to see how much information he'd press for. But Brian's poker face had snapped back in place and he simply clasped his hands on the table in front of him, waiting.

"The plan you proposed isn't going to save my mam, and we both know it. At best, it simply fails and poses a mild inconvenience to the Order. At worst, it gets her killed."

"You're asking me to risk my people's lives. We believe this is our best option for both keeping them safe and retrieving your mam."

I didn't bother to argue. Even if Brian genuinely thought that – which I doubted – it was off the cards.

"I will complete the Claiming for you –"

He stilled.

"– but we only if we do this my way."

"I'm listening."

Next to me, Teagan tensed. I resisted the urge to reach out and squeeze her hand and tell her it would be okay. We all knew my plan was batshit crazy and my words would be an empty promise, but we'd agreed before coming here that it was the only option that had a chance of ending this.

"I am going to contact Bannon and tell him I'm prepared to make the trade," I told Brian. "The Watchers will stay out of it. If, by some miracle, he releases my mam, Teagan and Pete will make sure she's brought somewhere safe. If he doesn't, at least we won't have shown our hand too early."

"And what if he kills her?"

My gut clenched in instinctual fear at the very words, but I held firm. "He won't. He'll use her for leverage to force me to complete the Claiming for him."

"You'll have to forgive my confusion because this all sounds like you intend to give the Order exactly what they want?"

"That's what we want them to think. The plan is simple. I distract them with the ritual while the Watchers surround the place and get my mam the hell out of there. Once you've done that, I'll complete the final steps of the Claiming that binds the magic to you, or a representative agreed upon in advance."

Brian leaned back in his chair, considering my proposal with his hands steepled beneath his chin. "And how do I know that you won't just betray us and take the magic for yourself?"

I'd expected the question, of course. Still, I gave an exasperated sigh. "Look, I'm not going to sit here and fawn at your feet. I don't trust you, and I don't trust the

Watchers. But I know this is bigger than me. You said it yourself that it's only a matter of time before knowledge of magic becomes mainstream. Neither of us want the Order in charge when that happens, and I am in no way equipped to deal with it myself. The Watchers are the logical choice here, and for all of our differences in opinion, I think your intentions are in the right place."

Brian inclined his head in acknowledgement of the truth in my words. He didn't immediately say no to my demands which I took as a win, but as the silence stretched between us, my nerves grew.

"I suppose you're not leaving me with much choice, are you?"

I stared him dead in the eye. "No. I'm not."

"I need to talk to the heads of the Watchers, but I think we can work with this. Once we have fine-tuned the details, of course."

"One more thing."

He folded his arms, and I got the distinct impression that he was at the edge of his patience.

"I need the sword back."

***

Things moved quickly once Brian got the green light from the mysterious heads of the Watchers. Within an hour, I was following Brian, alongside Teagan and Pete, through the winding corridors of the Watchers HQ, making our way down to the training facility. As we did, I cast surreptitious glances at my best friend to make sure she was still holding up okay.

Teagan had been having strange dreams and flashes of premonitions all night. Thankfully, she hadn't fully banshee'd out on us yet, but it seemed as though our futures were in a state of severe flux. Every decision we'd made from the moment I'd filled them in on my admittedly risky idea seemed to create a different possible outcome, and so far, none of them had been clear. The last thing we needed was to draw the Watcher's attention to how on edge her power was right now.

As we headed towards the observation room where the Watchers had conducted Teagan's "training", I spotted Kate hovering in the hallway. She was peering into one of the sterile white rooms, and it was clear from the way she was wringing her hands together that she was anxious. Frowning, I indicated with a subtle nod of my head for Teagan and Pete to continue on and I'd catch up.

I slowed to a stop and followed Kate's line of sight into the room. Jessie stood at the centre, her shoulders hunched as she faced what looked to be a makeshift straw target. I frowned.

"How's she getting on?" I asked, working hard to keep any judgement out of my tone.

Kate took her eyes off her niece for only a second to look at me, but it was enough for me to see her pinched lips and the tightness at the corner of her eyes.

"They've been running some ... tests. To figure out the best way to help her."

Tests. Right.

I watched as Jessie raised a trembling hand towards the target, only to drop it again. It was clear she wasn't in there willingly, and my heart ached for her. I knew what it was like to be afraid of your own magic, and I highly doubted that these so-called tests had the young girl's best interests at heart.

"Elemental magic isn't my strongest point," I said softly, "but if there's anything I can do to help, let me know."

Kate flashed me a grateful look that did little to ease the concern written all over her features. Casting a final glance into the white room, I left her to watch over her niece and prayed that the Watchers didn't do her any lasting psychological damage before they could be stopped.

I continued on to the observation room that the others had disappeared into. When I stepped inside, I found Brian in a heated discussion with Maggie while Pete and Teagan stood by, looking unimpressed.

"She can't be trusted," Maggie declared in no uncertain terms. And with that, she strode out of the room, casting me a withering glare as she passed.

I raised an eyebrow at Teagan who just shook her head, telling me not to bother asking.

So, we waited in tense silence for Maggie to return – presumably –with the sword I'd asked for. When she did, she walked straight past me and handed the long wooden box to Brian. A thrum of energy washed over me, bringing with it that inexplicable pull that reassured me she hadn't tried to trick us with an empty box.

Brian took the box, hesitating before he turned to me. "We stick to the plan."

I nodded.

"Don't fuck this up."

I didn't bother responding as I took the sword from him and awkwardly tucked it under one arm so I could pull my phone out of my pocket. Bannon's number was still in my recent calls list, and I hit the call button before I could rethink my life choices.

"Ms. O'Meara, I do hope you're not calling to cancel our meeting."

My grip tightened involuntarily on the phone, and I had to force myself to relax. "Actually, I'm calling to do you a favour. I'm ready to make the trade, but we both know that you're not holding my mam at the Order's old HQ. So, let's not waste each other's time. I'll meet you at the house in one hour."

Bannon chuckled. "Ah, you are well informed, I see. The change of venue is acceptable."

Fuck you and your acceptable.

"The ritual for my mam, that's the deal."

"Indeed."

"I'll see you in one hour."

CHAPTER TWENTY-FIVE

S weat ran down the back of my neck as I approached the large gates that barred entry to the white detached house. I shifted my grip on the long wooden box in my arms and allowed the hum of the sword's power to provide some comfort as it wrapped around me.

It was an effort not to look behind me to see if I could spot Teagan and Pete. I knew the two would be close by watching, but I'd made them promise not to intervene unless absolutely necessary – like guaranteed death necessary. That had earned me a full-on wolf growl from Pete as his instinct to protect warred with his understanding of what needed to be done, but I knew they'd stick to the plan.

Squaring my shoulders, I came to a stop in front of the two men who waited for me at the gates. There was an unmistakable glint of satisfaction in Bannon's steely eyes as he took in the box in my arms. Next to him,

Bill's expression was completely impassive, as if I was little more than an inconvenience to be dealt with so he could continue dusting ancient artefacts or robbing candy from babies. My mam was noticeably absent.

"Where is she?" I demanded.

"Waiting to see you." Bannon's smile brought to mind a shark closing in on its prey. "You'll be reunited as soon as we verify that you've brought the ritual."

Reunited didn't mean we'd be walking out of here together. It was a good thing we'd specifically planned for this double-cross, or I'd be feeling very stupid right now.

Without any signal from either of the men, a motor whirred and the gates behind them slowly opened. Just beyond them, I could see one of the stones that marked the boundary of the ward. I swallowed hard.

"Bill, if you'd be so kind as to relieve Ms. O'Meara of her baggage and escort her inside." Bannon stepped aside to allow us room to pass, and that self-satisfied glint in his eyes chilled me to my core.

Before I could protest, Bill closed the short distance between us. He yanked the sword box from me and wrapped a hand around my upper arm in a bruising grip. He half marched, half dragged me through the gates, not leaving me enough time to worry whether I'd make it through the lethal ward alive.

My ears gave an audible pop as we crossed the barrier. I wasn't sure whether I was relieved to be on the other side or not as I allowed myself one final look back. Then I fixed my gaze firmly forward and lifted my chin. I was here to do a job, and I was damn well going to do it.

Neither of the security guards stationed at the front of the house spared us a glance as Bill frogmarched me through the door and into a bright, spacious hallway. Three doors lined either side of a wide, sweeping staircase, and large double doors were visible at the rear. I couldn't see inside any of the rooms, but I took note of the layout nonetheless.

Directing me to the first door on our right, Bill pushed it open to reveal an office. The clean lines and modern decor were almost a mirror image of Bannon's office at the old Order HQ. It was anally neat and void of any kind of warmth. It said everything it needed to about the owner's personality. Warily, I made my way to the black leather chair facing the desk and sat down.

I could sense Bill looming behind me, but I pointedly ignored him as I drummed my nails on the desk's surface. Part of me itched to ask why they'd bothered to give me the sword at all if they were just going to take it back, but I refused to give him the satisfaction of my curiosity.

It was the best part of five minutes before Bannon deigned to join us. I had no doubt he saw it as some kind of power play, but I was just grateful for the chance to gather my thoughts. The head of the Order settled into the chair behind the desk and folded his hands in front of him, giving me an expectant look.

I held his hard stare, refusing to be cowed. "You're not getting anything from me until I see my mam." My mam might have been alive when I came here with Bres, but I needed to be sure that was still the case.

Bannon's eyes flicked over my shoulder to Bill and the other man moved to the wall, making me flinch. He hit a switch that I'd assumed to be a light switch, and the wooden panelling behind Bannon slid to the side to reveal a screen that covered most of the wall. Bannon pressed a button on the laptop resting next to him, and the screed flared to life.

An image of a spacious bedroom appeared behind him. In the corner, sitting at what appeared to be a cosy reading nook by the window, was my mam. She had a book in one hand and dainty tea cup in the other, and looked completely at home. Relief eased the tight knot of tension in my chest. Though it was disconcerting to see her looking so relaxed, it was preferable to her being a hysterical basket case, driven mad by the captivity that I was to blame for.

"As you can see, your mother has been well looked after." Bannon relaxed back in his chair. "In fact, I'm not sure she'll be in much of a hurry to leave."

I whipped my head around to glare at him. "You said you'd let her go. That was the deal."

"And we will ... when the time is right." All pretence of civility dropped from his expression. "Bill, can you be so kind as to check on Ms. O'Meara's mother to make sure she doesn't need anything?"

Fear rippled through me as Bill gave a curt nod and left the office.

"Now, I believe you have some information for me?"

I said nothing, my mouth going dry. Returning my attention to the screen, I watched as my mam looked up from her book a moment later. She smiled as the Order's so-called museum curator stepped into view.

Bannon watched me patiently, giving me the time needed for the unspoken threat to fully register.

"You've made your point." With tremendous effort, I tore my gaze away from the screen. "Let's talk."

***

Bannon spent an hour quizzing me on every aspect of the ritual, from timing to elements required to areas of risk. Unsurprisingly, he had all the necessary ingredients in place and ready to go, which led me to wonder just how much of the ritual he'd already known.

Eventually, he leaned forward and hit a button on his desk phone. "Can you please arrange some lunch for Ms. O'Meara and her mother in the lounge?"

He raised an eyebrow at the look of surprise on my face. "We want our esteemed guest to be comfortable, of course."

I didn't know what to say to that. There had been no question that I'd be expected to remain here until the Claiming was complete, but I'd fully expected him to dangle access to mam over me the whole time. Instead, he was organising a tea party for us?

A knock sounded on the office door, and I turned

as an honest-to-goodness butler stepped into the room. "If you'd be so kind as to follow me, ma'am."

Still clutching the wooden sword box, I did as he asked. We headed for a door on the opposite side of the hall, towards the rear of the house. He pushed it open and stepped aside, revealing a cosy lounge. A large stone fireplace formed the focal point for the room, and before it, a coffee table had been neatly laid out with a fine China tea set and a tiered platter filled with miniature cakes and sandwiches. Four high-backed chairs surrounded the table, and my mam sat daintily in one, teacup in hand. She looked up as I entered and gave me a wide smile.

"Aisling, darling, oh it's so good to see you."

She stood as, forgetting myself, I flew into the room and flung my arms around her. Chuckling, she patted my arm indulgently.

There was a soft clearing of the throat as the butler called our attention back to him. "Shall you require anything further?"

Extricating herself from my grip, my mam turned an adoring smile his way. "No, thank you, Henry. This is wonderful."

My eyebrows shot up so high I wouldn't have been surprised if they hit a different atmosphere. *Henry? What the hell?*

He gave a polite nod before turning on his heel and leaving us alone in the room. I sank into the chair closest to me, not sure my legs would hold me much longer if I got any more surprises.

"Are you okay? Have they hurt you?" I leaned forward as my mam returned to her seat opposite me. I couldn't see any signs of injury, but I had to be sure.

"Hurt me? Of course not. Whatever has you so wound up, Aisling? I know this whole stalker business is highly concerning." She chuckled almost girlishly and fanned herself with her hand. "I mean, can you believe someone thought *I* was worth stalking? But Declan and his whole party have been amazing. Who would have thought we actually had politicians who cared for the people?"

I opened my mouth and shut it again. There were no literally no words that could convey my confusion right now. What stalker? And who the hell was Dec–

My eyes widened. "Bannon?" I sputtered.

"Of course. Who else would I be referring to?" My mam picked up her teacup and took a delicate sip, eyeing me with a frown. "Really, Aisling, you are acting rather odd. Have you taken something?"

The laugh that bubbled up in my throat had me walking the edge of hysteria. I swallowed it back with effort. My mam didn't even realise she'd been kidnapped. I'd expected Bannon to play some kind of messed-up mind games, but this took the biscuit. All this time, I'd been going out of my mind with worry and she'd been here role-playing the damsel in distress to the Order's white-knight leader.

I shook my head. "Maybe my blood sugar levels are just low."

To cover my bafflement, I picked up one of the

small iced cakes from the tray and shoved it into my mouth. Maybe it was for the best that my mam had fallen for the Order's cover story. At least she didn't seem to be afraid. And considering they were unlikely to let her go anytime soon...

"Mam, did Bannon say how long you'd need to be here?"

She smiled, and I almost vomited with the hero worship that shone clear as day on her face. "He assures me the police are doing everything in their power to get it resolved. If we're lucky, it should be safe for me to return home again in two or three days. I am so glad he was able to bring you here to join me for lunch, though."

Just to emphasise the point, she picked up one of the smoked salmon and cream cheese finger sand-wiches and took a bite. She closed her eyes and hummed her pleasure before turning her attention back to me. "Now tell me, have you been seeing anyone lately? Time's ticking, you know. I'd like to be a young grandma."

CHAPTER TWENTY-SIX

Since my mam was under the impression that I was only visiting for lunch, I found myself unable to argue when Bill appeared to escort me out. I hugged her tightly and bid her a tearful farewell, earning myself an indulgent pat on the cheek. With a heavy heart, I followed Bill from the room.

"Bannon promised to let her go," I hissed once I was sure the door had closed fully behind me so my mam wouldn't overhear.

"And he will. So long as you co-operate."

He turned his back on me, clearly drawing a line under the conversation, and headed for the stairs. I followed in silence, knowing there was little point in arguing.

We made our way up to the second floor, but to my surprise, we didn't stop there. Bill pushed open a door on the left-hand side of the hallway to reveal yet another staircase. From what I'd seen of the outside of the house, I could only assume it led to the attic since there hadn't been a third floor. Really, he could have been leading me to a dungeon and it wouldn't have made a difference. I trudged up the steps behind him, head down and shoulders drooping as the weight of what I was doing truly hit me.

"Aisling? What the hell are you doing here?"

I snapped my head up at the sound of Bres's voice, belatedly realising that we'd reached the top of the stairs and emerged into what appeared to be a small living space in the converted attic.

Bres surged to his feet from the leather sofa that filled the centre of the room. He wore the same clothes as when I'd last seen him, and his eyes were wide with disbelief as he staggered towards us.

With an almost bored expression, Bill held out a hand and twisted it into a claw.

Bres let an agonised cry and crumpled to the ground, clutching his midsection. He writhed on the floor as his face turned a worrying shade of purple.

"Bres? Are you okay? What's wrong?" I ran to his side, dropping down next to him. "What are you doing to him?" I yelled at Bill. "You're hurting –"

My blood ran cold as the words died on my tongue. Bill's good eye, the one not covered by the patch, had turned entirely black. It was fixed on Bres and as he idly twisted his fingers, Bres's body bowed up of the floor, muscles visibly cording as his body strained against whatever was being done to it.

Bill blinked, his eye returning to its normal soulless

state as he dropped his hand back to his side. Bres's body fell limp to the floor and he curled in on himself, his breaths coming in shallow gasps.

The museum curator turned his attention on me. "Make yourself at home."

With that, he turned on his heel and disappeared down the stairs with clipped steps. A moment later, there was the audible sound of a lock clicking into place.

I sagged to the floor, my heart pounding against my chest as relief that he was gone made me weak. With a shuddery breath I turned my attention to Bres, who finally seemed to be breathing easier again. His eyes were still closed, tight with pain, but his skin was returning to a healthier colour.

"Are you okay?" I asked, rising to my knees so I could wrap an arm around him.

He took a couple of deep inhales before nodding. With an effort, and my help, he turned over to a sitting position, slumping back against the sofa. As he did, his t-shirt rode up, revealing a patchwork of purple and blue bruising all across his ribs.

I sucked in a breath.

He gave a feeble attempt at a wink. "Nothing a massage won't solve if you're offering."

Guilt and understanding hit me all at once. Something inside me cracked. "Have you... You've been here since the day you brought me to see my mam, haven't you?"

Oh god. Bile rose up in my throat at the realisation

that he'd been here all this time. I should've checked in on him. I'd been so caught up in finding the ritual, and I'd been so sure he'd gotten away. He was Bres, after all. He had more lives than a cat.

Bres reached out and tilted my chin up so that I was looking at him instead of staring in horror at the bruises covering his side. "Don't do that. You don't get to take the blame for my decisions. I could have refused to bring you here. Hell, I should've refused." He blew out a frustrated breath. "Maybe you wouldn't be here now if I had."

"You don't get to take the blame for my decisions," I parroted his words back at him, earning me a wry smile. "We both know the Order would have gotten their hands on me one way or the other. At least this way, it's on my terms."

Curiosity glinted in his blue eyes, but he glanced warily around and I realised we were likely being monitored. I'd need to watch what I said.

"Are you able to stand?" I asked, figuring we might as well make ourselves comfortable since we'd likely be here for a while.

Bres nodded, and I helped to brace his weight as we rose from the floor. He failed to completely hide his wince of pain and his legs buckled slightly as he stood, but we made it onto the sofa without falling over. I took the chance to scan him, looking for any more signs of injury.

"What is he?" I asked. "Bill."

"Evil."

There was a numbness to his tone that told me whatever history lay between the two men wasn't a pleasant one and wasn't one Bres wanted to elaborate on. I was tempted to push further, but now wasn't the time.

"Why did they keep you here?" I said, turning my attention back to our current situation. "Why not just send you on your way with a warning?"

"For the pleasure of my company?"

I folded my arms and waited, in no mood for making light of the situation.

He sighed and looked away. "It seems daddy dearest has known about my intentions to screw up his world domination plans for quite some time. He was happy to humour me while it suited his purposes. Now, he intends to sacrifice me to solidify his bond to the magic and teach me the error of my ways."

"Daddy dearest?" Realisation dawned on me and my eyes shot wide. "Bannon? Bannon is your dad?"

"Lucky me, huh."

I shook my head, trying to make sense of what he was saying. Bannon was his father?

"The ritual doesn't call for a sacrifice," I protested. At least not a physical one, anyway.

Bres gave a bitter laugh. "It's the Order. A party's not complete for them without a little bloodshed."

"But you're his son." Disbelief made the words come out as a whisper. I couldn't fathom it, couldn't wrap my head around the logic that somebody would be willing to sacrifice their own flesh and blood – even someone as evil as Bannon.

"Yeah, well, I come from a long line of dickheads, it seems."

My chest clenched at the resignation in his tone as he let his head drop back against the sofa. It was like all the fight had left him. How could he not be angry that his own dad was doing this to him? He'd been so hellbent on getting revenge for his mam, and now he was just ... sitting here.

"So, that's it? You're just giving up?"

He glanced sideways at me. "Is that not what you're doing? You're here too, in case you hadn't noticed."

"No!"

I couldn't say more than that with the risk somebody might be listening, but I put every ounce of my determination into that one word, willing him to see the fire that still blazed inside me – blazed even stronger now after what he'd just told me.

He searched my face. I had no idea what he was looking for, but it felt like he was seeing right through me, seeing all of me, and it was an effort not to flinch away so that he didn't see the bad parts of me as well as the good. He reached out to cup my cheek, and I stayed completely still, a mess of emotions warring within me.

After an endless moment, he dropped his hand and looked away, casting his gaze down.

"It wouldn't have mattered if I'd been the golden child. Bannon was always going to sacrifice me," he admitted quietly. "He sees it as repayment for a betrayal my family committed a long time ago. My ancestor – my namesake, I guess – was manipulating the Fomorians. He was helping them to prepare for the Claiming, but in truth he intended to the destroy the magic at the point of the ritual when the magic was at its most vulnerable. The Tuatha's sacrifice put an end to his plan, but the Order have never forgotten."

I froze, my stomach dropping. So he had known about his ancestor's plan. Did that mean Killian was right about everything else?

"You're not your ancestor." Please let that be true. Please let me not be wrong about him.

Bres gave a snort of derision. "Am I any better than them? For a long time after my mam's death, I thought that was exactly the kind of revenge I wanted. To destroy the magic. To watch Bannon have everything that he desired within reaching distance and to be the one who ripped it from him."

My chest ached at the self-loathing thick in his voice. He had been beaten down for so long that he couldn't even begin to see the possibility of good in himself. But it was there; I knew it was.

"You thought you wanted that. So, what do you want now? What changed?"

He raised his head, and the raw emotion in his eyes stole my breath away.

"I met you. You helped me see that there were good people in this world who would try to do the right thing, no matter what it cost them. I realised that if I followed in my ancestor's footsteps, I'd be no better than Bannon. Magic isn't good or evil. It's us who make it that way. Who would I be if I destroyed that potential for good?"

"So, you don't want to destroy the magic?"

He shook his head. "I was honest with you when I said I wanted you to Claim it. Destroying the magic would be preferable to the Order getting their hands on it. But you gave me hope that there was another way."

He held up a hand to stop any protest I might make. "I know you don't want to Claim it, and I've accepted your decision. But for however long I have left, I'm going to hold on to that hope because I need to know she didn't die for nothing and that there's a future where evil doesn't win."

CHAPTER TWENTY-SEVEN

The next two days passed in a haze. Every couple of hours I would try to unlock the attic door using my elemental lock-picking trick, but it was clear the Order had more than just a key keeping the door closed. While staying here was part of my plan, Bres being sacrificed by his own father most definitely was not. With each failed attempt, my frustration and desperation grew.

Bres, for his part, seemed unbothered by his impending fate. Instead, he focused his attentions on the small, fully stocked kitchen. Despite my protests about him being injured and needing to rest, he insisted on cooking for us both. I woke each morning to a freshly cooked breakfast and sat down each evening to a mouth-watering three-course meal.

Somehow, in spite of the situation we found ourselves in, we talked and laughed easily as we passed the hours together. Bres told me about the adventures his mam would invent for them, and I told him about my mam, about her head-in-the-clouds, full of life ways, and how she had eagerly bought into the suspense novel story Bannon had painted for her. Conscious of the fact we were likely being monitored, we avoided discussing the Claiming again after that initial conversation, but really there wasn't anything more to say.

By some unspoken agreement, we spent the nights together too. The converted space included two bedrooms and a bathroom as well as the living area, but it seemed neither of us wanted to be alone in the dark. When I helped Bres to bed that first night, insisting that I check his injuries properly, he'd taken my hand and asked me to stay. I hadn't said no.

So, we'd slept side by side, and when the night-mares came, I huddled into him and let his warmth soothe the crippling fear of what was to come.

The dreamscape and Killian were noticeably absent on the lead-up to the eclipse. I didn't know if it was because of Bres's presence, because of where I was, or because the dreamscape was fading. The cowardly part of me was relieved not to have to face Killian knowing I'd be ultimately responsible for his death, but the thought of not seeing him before this was all over made my heart ache.

Bill returned just as we sat down to dinner on the evening before the eclipse. Bres had prepared an impressive spread of steaks, salad, and baked potatoes, and an apple crumble was warming in the oven.

The museum curator took in the plates laid out on the table before fixing his soulless stare on Bres. "The Guardian needs her rest. You'll stay in the basement tonight."

I opened my mouth to protest, but Bres gave me a smile that didn't quite reach his eyes. "It's okay. He's right. You have a big day tomorrow."

His eyes lingered on my face for a moment, and I had a sense that he wanted to say more. Setting his jaw, he turned and made his way to Bill's side. When the other man moved to grip his arm, he shook him off.

"I know the way."

The two men disappeared down the stairs and the door slammed shut behind them, leaving me alone.

I stared numbly at the beautiful meal Bres had prepared. The hollowness in the pit of my stomach had nothing to do with the hunger that had only moments ago had me anticipating my first bite of the succulent steak. Now, even the thought of eating made bile rise up the back of my throat.

I pushed away from the table and stood.

Feeling completely and utterly lost, I made my way to the bedroom I'd shared with Bres for the last couple of nights. As I curled up on my side on the bed and hugged his pillow to me, the first sob broke free.

The nightmares came for me. The eclipse and a never-ending darkness. Me screaming a silent scream as

Bannon sacrificed Bres with a cruel smile twisting his features. Killian's agony as the dreamscape imploded. By the time I woke the next morning to the sound of the door opening, I was grateful for the reprieve.

Bill didn't bother knocking before he pushed open the bedroom door and I jolted upright, hugging the covers tight to me.

"Get dressed. It's time to go." He turned and strode out of the room without waiting to see if I'd comply.

Exhaustion weighed heavy on me as I dragged myself out of bed. It took far less time than I'd have liked to get ready, and I reluctantly joined Bill in the living area a few minutes later.

The museum curator scanned me from head to toe, then turned on his heel without a word. I followed him in silence, each step I took rattling through my bones like a death knell.

After a couple of days confined to the attic with only small windows to allow in daylight, it was a shock to step outside and take in the clear blue sky. The sun shone overhead, and at the edge of it, I could have sworn I caught a hint of darkness. When I blinked, it was gone, but the sense of trepidation remained.

A line of cars idled outside the house, ready to bring us to the ritual site. Armed guards stood next to each of them, and I frowned as I noted that all the cars were the same gunmetal grey colour.

Hadn't Richie said the car that hit Pete was black?

A lingering question niggled at the back of my mind, but I pushed the thought away. I had bigger things to worry about right now. Still, I filed it away to come back to later – assuming I survived the next few hours, of course.

With a none-too-gentle nudge, Bill directed me to one of the cars in the centre of the line. I hesitated, walking slowly in the hopes that I would catch sight of my mam or Bres. Unfortunately, Bill wasn't feeling too patient. He put a hand on the back of my head and shoved me into the back seat of the car, slamming the door before I could even react.

"Ms. O'Meara," Bannon greeted me, his hands clasped in his lap as he sat across from me, looking far too relaxed. "I hope you're well rested. We've an exciting day ahead."

I slumped into the seat and closed my eyes.

The drive to the Church of the Blessed Heart was both painfully short and the longest of my life. I was surprised to see that the Order had managed to set up roadblocks about a mile out from the site. It made sense that they would want to control access to the area so we weren't disturbed, but why weren't the police asking questions? Was this what political clout bought you?

Trepidation tightened my muscles as I climbed out of the car at the entrance to the church grounds. I didn't know if it was my imagination, but the signs of life seemed more pronounced as we made our way through the graveyard and past the old ruins of the church. I catalogued each patch of new growth as I walked, using it as a distraction against the thumping of my heart. New life. Hope. I clung to the thought with everything I had.

The Order had clearly been busy this morning, and armed guards moved about the green field beyond the church's boundary walls, making preparations. I scanned them but stopped counting once I'd hit thirty guards. My panic level began to rise.

It was fine. The Watchers had numbers on their side too. The plan would still work.

Doubts started to creep in as I climbed over the low stone wall and followed Bannon to the edge of the illusion spell that blocked the field's true appearance from view.

"If you'd be so kind as to do the honours?" Bannon held out his arm to me, and I blinked in confusion at it. "The illusion," he clarified. "You will need to take us across."

Of course, because only those of Tuatha blood could cross the illusion spell. Those with Tuatha blood or those with more of Bres's magic dirt. I guessed Bannon wasn't in the mood to get his hands dirty.

Trying not to cringe at the thought of touching him, I placed my fingertips lightly on his arm and took the final steps that would bring us across.

Seven large standing stones appeared before us, forming a circle around a large patch of scorched earth. A glance up showed me an ominously grey sky despite the fact that the sun still shone brightly on the other side of the illusion. A black sphere had appeared at the edge of the sun, and I knew it was only a matter of time before it swallowed the light completely. I shivered.

More members of the Order milled about here, making preparations for the ritual. But that wasn't what made my heart freeze in my chest.

Two figures were tied to the standing stones furthest away from me. While Bres looked oddly relaxed despite the bindings that no doubt cut into his skin, my mam looked like she was about to faint on the stone next to him. She had a gag covering her mouth, presumably to stop her from screaming hysterically, and her eyes were wide with panic. It was how I'd expected to find her when I handed myself over to the Order, but as much as I'd expected it, seeing it was a whole different ball game.

"Why is she here?" I demanded.

"Insurance."

I balled my hands into tight fists, my body shaking with the effort of holding myself in place when all I wanted to do was lunge for him and tear out his throat. This was what we'd expected, I reminded myself, fighting to remain calm.

"You will set up in the centre," Bannon instructed before striding away, clearly confident that I would obey.

I inhaled deeply and held it for a count of three before releasing it. Anger still burned through my veins, but I forced myself to release the tension in my hands and made my way to the centre of the stone circle.

Four objects had been laid out on the ground in preparation. The sword, no longer encased in its protective wooden box, appeared to glow where it rested on the scorched earth. Next to it lay a simple wooden spear with a gleaming metal point. A jagged piece of stone roughly the size of my hand sat beside it, the rough edges of strange carvings visible on its surface. The power that emanated from them almost stole my breath. But it was the fourth object that sent me to my knees.

Dagda's cauldron.

The small cast iron cauldron rested on the ground before me. The energy that hummed within it was both intimately familiar and strangely alien as my magic mixed with Dub and Carmen's at its centre.

This power would be the catalyst for the ritual. So, why did I feel only relief as I reached out to touch the artefact?

Runes flared to life along the surface as my fingers brushed the edge of the cauldron. I snapped my hand back and the runes disappeared, but their image was etched into my mind.

"Thirty minutes," Bannon declared, his voice ringing out across the space.

With a shaky breath, I stood and squared my shoulders. There was no going back now.

CHAPTER TWENTY-EIGHT

The clock ticked down, marking the minutes as what was left of my normal life faded away. I took a moment to look around me, mapping out where everyone was stationed and where the areas of risk were. My eyes locked onto Bill, who was walking a circle from standing stone to standing stone.

What was he doing?

I frowned as he dropped something on the ground between two of the large stones. He moved to the next and did the same thing again.

Shit. Was he laying out a ward?

My heart raced as the implications struck me. If the ward he was laying was the same as the one at the house, nobody would be able to get through. Even trying would kill them.

Oh god. Teagan. Pete. I had no way of warning them. And my mam, she'd be stuck here inside this circle, at Bannon's mercy if he even got a hint that I was planning to betray him.

My chest tightened as these thoughts hit me, one after the other. Each one made it harder to think straight, and panic threatened to take hold.

Then movement to the left of my mam caught my eye. Momentarily distracted, I turned my attention to the standing stone where Bres hung.

Bres's face was carefully blank and it took a moment for me to spot what was out of place. His right leg was stretched to the far edge of the stone, his bindings strained. He looked up, meeting my questioning gaze, then cast a quick glance at Bill who had almost completed his circle.

Once he was sure the museum curator wasn't paying attention, Bres stretched his leg another couple of inches and with a quick jerk, kicked something on the ground next to him. Understanding dawned on me as a stone went skittering backwards across the grass – effectively breaking Bill's ward circle.

Bres gave me a cheeky wink before resuming his position on the stone, looking completely and utterly bored.

Relief rippled through me, and my racing heart calmed enough for me to breathe again. There was still a chance. We could still do this.

I held that thought firmly in my mind as I set the artefacts in their required places. The shard of Liath Fáil I placed on the ground, facing north. The sword and spear I impaled into the earth to the southwest and southeast respectively. Then taking the cauldron, I stood in the centre of the triangle the three artefacts formed.

At some point as I'd been getting everything ready, the light had changed to a cold, silvery hue. An unnatural silence had fallen and even the wind had stilled. I looked up to find a solid black disc now covering three quarters of the sun's surface and an odd twilight bathing the sky.

Bannon moved to the top of the triangle, facing me. Bill stood behind him with his hands clasped, and the rest of the men moved to stand guard between the standing stones.

Bannon swept his arms wide and turned to look at them all, as if addressing his parish from a pulpit. "It is time," he declared, his voice filling the space. "Today, we will right the wrongs done to our forefathers. The Order will ascend to true greatness."

At his words, the light dimmed. The large standing stones cast elongated shadows, somehow all aimed inwards. Towards me.

Holding my breath, I looked up and stared as, bit by bit, the moon devoured the final inches of the sun.

One heartbeat. Two.

Darkness flooded the land.

A burning ring of fire hung suspended above me. My hands tightened on the cauldron in my grip, and I stared at it, both mesmerised and completely and utterly terrified.

Without making the conscious decision to do so, I

began speaking the words of the ritual. They flowed from my lips, a language unknown to me and yet integral to every strand of my DNA. Even if I'd wanted to stop them, I couldn't.

Dagda's cauldron heated to my touch and runes flared to life around its surface. Power crackled over my skin, flowing over me and down into the earth.

A strange white glow formed beneath my feet, growing in strength with each inhale I took. White lines spread from that point, reaching out to the artefacts that surrounded me. My voice rose higher, and the lines joined together to form a blazing triquetra all around me.

A vicious wind whipped up from the edges of the symbol. It rose up, encasing me in a vortex and blocking all else from view. My hair lashed at my face, and its bite was so sharp that I was convinced my skin was being flayed from my bones.

Then, in a silent flash, power exploded from the cauldron.

White light filled the space. It was the beginning, the end, the everything and nothing. I stood there at the centre of it. Alone.

The cauldron was no longer in my grasp, and as I reached out a hand before me, I was surprised to find I even had substance. Surely I had just shattered into billions of atoms and was now standing in the afterlife?

I moved my hand from side to side, surprised to see that a rainbow-like reflection followed my movements. It lasted only a moment before fading back to white. It was energy, I realised. The magic that filled this space and had been slowly growing in strength ever since the summer solstice.

But it wasn't complete.

Turning in a slow circle, I was suddenly certain that there was more to this place than what I was seeing. Where the whiteness had moments ago seemed never-ending, I now caught the flicker of shadows on the periphery. Empty spaces waiting to be filled with magic. Magic I needed to draw from the dreamscape.

Killian's face flashed before my eyes, and I sucked in a breath. The sound of his agonised cries from my dreams the night before were as fresh as if they were happening now. Were they doomed to become a reality? My throat burned at the thought.

It didn't matter that he'd told me this was what he wanted. It didn't matter that the magic would return sooner or later, even without my assistance. The idea of being responsible for his death was almost crippling, and to think that his death might be one of pain and suffering was too much to bear.

Closing my eyes, I let the grief consume me. A minute. That was all I'd give myself to mourn.

And after that minute was done, I straightened. I dug down deep for the strength I needed to do this, and I made the only promise I could. "I won't let it be for nothing."

With that solemn vow, I turned my focus inwards to the power that waited at my core. Now that I was paying attention to it, I could sense the tethers that connected me to the energy all around me. There were weaker strands too, stretching far into the distance to the magic waiting to return. Those were the strands I focused on now.

I called the magic to me, urging it to fill the empty spaces and take its rightful place within the fabric that made us who we are. It came without resistance.

Power crashed over me. It struck in a deluge that shattered my very being, making and unmaking me in one single moment. It flowed through me, using me as a conduit to return to our world. I couldn't breathe, couldn't speak, couldn't see.

Desperately, I clung on, some deep part of my consciousness yelling at me that I had to live to complete the ritual or this would all have been for nothing. I latched onto that thought and clenched my fists, roaring as the magic flooded through me. I could do this. I had to do this.

My vision darkened around the edges, and I swayed on my feet. The last thing I remembered was the sound of my scream. Then everything went black.

CHAPTER TWENTY-NINE

Consciousness returned to me slowly, and when it did, I blinked in confusion. I was no longer suspended in an endless white. Instead, I found myself sitting on a cushion of lush grass in the centre of a meadow. Not just any meadow, but at the heart of the dreamscape.

Darkness filled the space, and I looked up, surprised to see that it was nighttime. The cracks that had split the sky on my previous visits were gone, and in their place hung a huge moon. It was an odd rust colour, and it bathed the entire space in an eerie reddish tone.

I'd known the ritual would fold time to bring the three eclipses into line, but it hadn't occurred to me that they might not align on the same plane of existence. Now as I looked up at the lunar eclipse, I wondered if this meant I'd miraculously made it to the second stage.

As the thought occurred to me, a figure came into view, moving towards me with what looked like a sword in their hand.

Frowning, I rose to my feet.

As the person closed the gap between us, their features grew clearer. My mouth dropped open as I took in the long blonde hair and familiar green eyes. If I didn't know better, I'd swear I was looking at a reflection. But this reflection was holding a sword that I clearly remembered planting into the ground back at the ritual site. And I? Well, I stood here defenceless.

"Who are you?" I asked, shocked to find my voice steady and clear.

The other me tilted her head and assessed me. "I am you. I am the possibility of what could be and the threat of what may come to pass."

"Do you go around carrying swords all the time?" I swallowed, eyeing the blade nervously.

"Claíomh Solas is judgement. It sees truth where lies seek to mislead. It sees honour where evil seeks to hold sway. Speak your truth and be judged."

Speak my what?

Was this my trial? The woman in my vision had promised that I'd know what to do when the time came, but standing here now I felt like I was about to take a test I hadn't studied for. What truth was I supposed to give? Yes, I did accidentally break my cousin's unicorn bracelet when I was eight and blamed it on her brother?

Panic clouded my thoughts as I imagined falling at

the very first hurdle. I pushed it back. I had gotten this far – I could figure it out.

The sword was intended to judge me and my intentions. Okay, great. What could I say that would be the most truthful way of answering that question?

I searched deep inside myself, seeking the words that made me uncomfortable to even think. The truth was rarely comfortable, and if I was going to be judged, I needed to be as honest as possible. Even if that honesty wasn't pretty.

"I'm a murderer," I said finally. "My mistakes have cost people their lives. But worse than that, I have taken lives with my own hand. I feel it like a black stain on my soul every day, and I sometimes wonder if I really am the good guy in this story. I don't deserve to be the Guardian, and I definitely shouldn't be the one deciding the fate of magic. That is my truth."

Shame heated my cheeks but I kept my chin up. I would own my actions. Even if it meant the magic deemed me unworthy, I would own them.

My shadow self moved faster than my eyes could track. She pulled back her sword, and drove it straight through me.

My hands flew to my midsection, and my eyes flared wide with shock as the blade punctured my flesh. I looked down in horror, but before I could utter even a cry of pain, the sword began to glow and a warm light bathed me.

The world flared white again and when it faded, I found myself once more standing in the darkened world of the dreamscape. Only, instead of being impaled by the sword, it was now gripped tightly in my hand.

Blinking in confusion, I straightened. No blood stained my clothes or my hands, and no pain registered. It was almost as if I hadn't just been stabbed with a really pointy sword.

My shadow self stood before me, her expression every bit as unreadable as it had been earlier. "You speak true," she intoned. "And so you pass to the next trial."

I opened my mouth to utter a smart remark about the warning being appreciated this time, but snapped it closed again as a spear appeared in her hand.

Only pure instinct allowed me to block the strike that she aimed at my head. The spear rebounded off the sword's blade, sending a jolt of pain through my arm. I stumbled backwards, trying to put distance between myself and the weapon.

My mistake quickly became apparent with the next flurry of strikes. The spear's reach far surpassed that of my sword and I was driven back further, forced to defend in any way I could.

Clumsily I parried with the sword, almost dropping it more than once. It was fear and desperation rather than skill that had me diving to the side when the spear tip came within inches of my body. This bitch was going to kill me.

It continued like that, her striking, and me staying alive by sheer dumb luck. More than one of her strikes managed to slice through my flesh, and blood mingled with sweat, soaking my skin. My muscles ached from the unfamiliar weight of the sword, and I was only just managing to keep it raised. I wanted to stop. I wanted to hold my hands up in surrender. But I couldn't. I had to keep going.

An unexpected wallop to the side of my leg sent me stumbling to one knee, the sword clattering to the ground as I reached out to stop myself.

"Do you yield?"

I looked up to find Declan Bannon standing over me, holding the spear with the tip pointed squarely at my chest. Some part of me knew it wasn't really him, but fury crashed through me nonetheless as I stared up at his sneering face.

"No!"

With immense effort, I pushed back up to standing, gritting my teeth as the spear's tip pressed into my sternum. If I was to die here, I would not die on my knees. Not in front of this man.

The image flickered. Bannon's features shifted and changed until my shadow self stood before me once more. The spear disappeared.

"You fight valiantly," she said. "Though the odds are stacked against you, you stand with honour in the hope that good will endure."

I glared at her. What normal person wouldn't fight back when someone was trying to stick them like a pig? It had nothing to do with good versus evil. It was simple survival. Yes, the thought of Bannon winning had driven me to my feet when I'd have gladly surrendered, but what sane person would want that evil megalomaniac to...

Oh.

Had that actually been what drove me? The thought of evil succeeding?

As I considered the possibility, the ground in front of me began to shimmer. Dagda's cauldron appeared at my feet and I took an involuntary step back.

Unease prickled my skin as I stared at the artefact. Back in the real world, there'd been no mistaking the aura of power that emanated from the cauldron. But here in the dreamscape, I could actually see the magic contained within its depths. Inky black swirls wound their way through opalescent mists that invited you to get lost within them. It was the dark tendrils that stole my attention, however.

"These artefacts were born of Tuatha magic," my shadow self said. "They were never meant to contain that which is not natural to our lands. The same will be true of the earth on which your mortal body stands."

I frowned, tearing my gaze from the cauldron to look at her in confusion. "I don't understand."

"Foreign magics reside inside the cauldron and in the power that awaits return. It does not belong to your homeland, and the effects of its release are unknown."

"Foreign magic?" Realisation dawned as I watched the inky swirls dance like shadows across the cauldron's surface. "You mean Dub and Carmen's magic."

She nodded. "It will return just like the rest of the magic, and if you let it, it will combine with the magic you bind and change it. The magic will become something new."

A cold dread spread through my veins as I considered the implications. "Something evil?"

For the first time, my shadow self smiled. "Magic is neither good nor evil. It just is. What this new change will bring, I cannot tell you. I can only tell you that it will happen. You must make the decision."

"What decision?" I asked, my brow furrowing. For some reason, I didn't think putting the genie back in the bottle was an option.

"Let the release take its natural course and let Ireland's magic become something new. Or don't. Siphon the foreign magic and bind it to yourself. Act as its vessel and guard it."

I gaped at her. She wanted me to take Dub and Carmen's magic inside myself?

The memory of siphoning Dain and Dothar's life force assaulted me. I squeezed my eyes shut and tried to block out the image of their glassy eyes, the feeling of their magic washing through me. Every part of me believed that I had stained my soul with that action – I'd told her as much not so long ago. What would it mean if I took Dub and Carmen's magic into me too?

But more importantly, what would it mean if I didn't?

Bres's words of a few nights ago echoed in my head,

mirroring those of my shadow self. *Magic isn't good or evil. It's us who make it that way.*

He'd said I'd changed his mind, that I'd given him hope for the potential for good that existed while the magic remained. Could I hold on to that hope now? Could I be the anchor for good that he believed me to be?

I wasn't sure, but I knew I wanted to be.

With a trembling hand, I reached out towards the cauldron. Once more, my eyes locked onto those inky swirls. And I called them to me.

CHAPTER THIRTY

Shadows engulfed me and the world went black. I was falling, falling, falling. Then everything snapped into focus.

I was back in the dreamscape with the soft grass once more cushioning me where I sat. It was daytime now and the sun shone in the clear blue sky above me, warming my skin. My shadow self was nowhere to be seen, but when I looked down, I found the shard of Liath Fáil resting in my lap.

Warily, I picked up the stone, turning it from side to side. Jagged markings roughened its side, and a shiver ran through me as I ran my finger along its edge.

Was this another test? Had these people never heard of instructions?

Soft footsteps crunched in the grass nearby, and I jerked my head up. Killian was walking towards me, a ghost of a smile on his lips as he looked completely at ease in his black jeans and t-shirt. All signs of the exhaustion that had plagued him were gone, and he looked exactly like he had the first time we met.

I leapt to my feet and ran to him, flinging my arms around him and almost knocking him over.

He chuckled and squeezed me tightly, lifting me off the ground as he did. After a long moment, he set me back down and held me at arm's length. He scanned me from head to toe, something like pride shining in his eyes.

"You've done well, Guardian."

I shook my head, still too shocked to see him to pay much attention to the compliment. "Are you better? How are you here? I thought I'd siphoned all the magic."

He gestured for me to sit, settling himself down on the ground next to me. His presence at my side was as warm and reassuring as it always had been, but when he looked up at the clear sky, there was no mistaking the concern that darkened his eyes.

"You did," he said finally. "I guess you could say we're suspended at a moment in time. The eye of the storm."

The surge of hope I'd felt at seeing him alive and well burst like a balloon struck by a pin, and I dropped my gaze to my lap. "So you're not better."

"If you mean am I going to survive what's been put in motion, then no. I'm sorry for the pain that causes you, Aisling. But please know that this is my choice, and I'm at peace with it."

I swallowed past the lump that had suddenly

wedged itself in my throat and raised my eyes to look at him. "So this is goodbye?"

Killian nudged my shoulder gently. "Let's think of it as graduating. You haven't been a half bad student actually. You've come a long way from the clueless girl who stumbled blindly into the world of magic."

I choked out a laugh. "Clueless is one way to put it."

He sighed. "I wish I had more time to prepare you for the future you face. You carry a world of potential within you, and you've only just scratched the surface of what you will become."

Potential. There was that word again.

"What happens now?" I asked quietly.

Killian indicated to the stone resting in my lap. "Liath Fáil once heralded the reign of our greatest kings and leaders. Use it to help the magic find its rightful place."

The light around us dimmed and the shadows cast by the trees at the edge of the meadow elongated, reaching towards us like clawed fingers. I looked up the see a dark shape appearing at the edge of the sun's surface.

Killian turned to me and took my hand in his, a grim urgency tightening his features. "When you return to your world, the magic will be untethered, more powerful than anything you could ever imagine. You must be prepared. Claim the magic or bind it before the eclipse is complete. If you don't, it will destroy you."

"Oh, no pressure so," I muttered. "How long do we have before..."

I wasn't ready to say goodbye yet. But the meadow was growing darker around us, and I knew that above me, the moon was devouring the sun inch by inch in the third and final eclipse. We were running out of time.

"Not long," Killian said softly, squeezing my hand. His eyes glistening in the dim light and I swallowed hard. "I'm proud of you, Aisling. You may not have wanted the role of Guardian, but you were made for it. Whatever happens, remember who you are and the strength that flows in your veins. Trust in it and trust in yourself."

Tears burned my eyes, and I bit down hard on my lip to stop them from falling. "I'm going to miss you."

Killian reached out and wrapped his arms around me, pulling me into a tight hug. "Thank you for setting me free," he whispered.

And then darkness fell.

The darkness shattered into chaos. I was back at the ritual site, standing in the centre of the glowing triquetra. The wind had stilled, but yells of surprise were coming from all around me, and as lightning forked through the still dark sky, I spotted people swarming the field beyond the stone circle.

My head swam as I tried to make sense of what was

happening. Where was Killian? Was the dreamscape gone?

I pushed the thought from my mind and fought to ground myself in the here and now. Killian's warning rang in my mind even as a tentative hope surged at the possibility that help had arrived.

At the head of the triquetra, Bannon's expression was thunderous. "Guard her," he snarled to Bill. "I will deal with this."

I paid him little heed as he strode away, my attention locked onto the shard of Liath Fáil resting on the ground mere feet from where he'd been. How had it gotten there? It had been in my lap only moments ago in the dreamscape.

Without thinking, I lunged for the stone. Sharp, agonising pain jolted through me, and I crashed to my knees.

I ground my teeth against the pain and looked up to find Bill watching me with an impassive expression and that terrifying all-black eye. His hand was raised towards me, and as he twisted his clawed fingers, every nerve in my body screamed. My back bowed.

A vicious growl came from somewhere to my left. A huge brown wolf soared through the air and smashed into Bill. The museum curator tumbled out of sight, the wolf right on his heels.

I gasped in relief as the onslaught of pain suddenly ceased. Ghostly echoes of it rippled through me, gradually reducing in intensity until I could breathe again.

From where I knelt on the ground, my fingers

digging into the hard earth, I raised my head and took in the scene around me. Watchers had swarmed the area and were engaging the Order in various forms of combat. Lights flared, mingling with intermittent flashes of lightning from above, and gunshots were swallowed by booms of thunder. It was mayhem.

Conscious that time was something I didn't have the luxury of, I scanned the area until I spotted Teagan and Brian moving between the shadows. They were making a beeline for my mam and had a clear path ahead of them. I rose to my knees, willing them to hurry.

As I kept my gaze fixed on them, I crawled towards the stone I needed to complete the binding. I was within inches of the artefact when Brian finally cut the ropes that bound my mam and a figure I recognised as Eamonn appeared at their side to carry her to safety.

Relief made my arms weak and I almost collapsed to the ground. Then Teagan turned my way. And her eyes were glowing a terrifying purple.

No! We were so close.

My panicked gaze darted to Bres, still bound to the stone next to where my mam had been. Teagan followed my line of sight and gave me a sharp nod.

With a growing sense of urgency, I lunged for the shard of Liath Fáil.

My fingers had barely closed around it when a perfectly shined black shoe slammed down on my hand. I roared in pain as my grip involuntarily loosened on the stone.

The owner of the shoe grabbed a chunk of my hair and yanked my head back. I looked up into Bill's emotionless black eye. Deep red gashes covered one side of his face, and I could've sworn I caught a flash of bone beneath the jagged flesh.

"Bannon should've killed you when he had the chance," he sneered, showering me in bloody spittle.

Terror froze me in place. If Bill was here, where was Pete?

The thought had barely flashed into my mind when Brian stepped up on Bill's right. He held a gun in his hand, and he drove the butt of it into the museum curator's temple.

Bill's grip on me released, but not before he tore clumps of hair from my head, sending pain blazing across my scalp. The blow knocked him backward.

Right into the jaws of a waiting wolf.

CHAPTER THIRTY-ONE

I watched in a combination of horror and fascination as Pete tore Bill's throat out. Even Brian, who was reaching out a hand to help me to my feet, turned a bit green at the sight.

Taking the offered help, I rose from the ground, my legs shaky beneath me. My hand throbbed and my scalp burned, but more than that, an odd pressure seemed to be building behind my sternum. It pressed against my rib cage, swelling outward to the point that it was getting harder to breathe.

I didn't have to look up to know we were running out of time, but I did anyway. A thin sliver of light was visible at the edge of the moon's sphere. The sun was fighting back against the darkness.

"Transfer the magic to me, Aisling," Brian urged as he held the shard of Liath Fáil out to me. "Now, while we have the chance."

Tearing my attention from the ticking clock above

our head, I took the stone from him. I hesitated as I met his trusting gaze and wondered if I was truly doing the right thing.

A flash of lighting scorched the sky, momentarily stealing my vision and sending a searing pain through my skull. I clutched my head, dimly aware of someone calling my name. Squinting against the pain, I could just about make out Teagan and Bres running towards us. I blinked, trying to bring everything back into focus.

"Don't do it, Aisling," Bres called. "They can't be trusted."

Brian whipped his head around and scowled at Bres's words, but before he could say anything, a figure loomed up like a nightmare behind Bres.

Bannon grabbed Bres from behind and locked an arm around him. He held a vicious-looking dagger and had the blade pressed against the soft flesh of Bres's throat before I could scream a warning.

"That's right, Ms. O'Meara." Bannon addressed me with his usual, unshakeable calm. "We wouldn't want you making any rash decisions."

Teagan skidded to a stop a few feet away from them. Her expression was torn as she looked from Bres and Bannon to me. In the dim light, her eyes seemed to flicker back and forth between that eerie glow and her natural colour, and if the tense set of her body was any indication, she couldn't act without detrimental consequences.

I gave her the slightest shake of my head and then fixed my attention on Bannon.

"Let him go. I have the stone and I'm ready to do the transfer." I held up the shard of Liath Fáil so he could clearly see it.

A loud rumble of thunder rolled through the sky, and I had to grit my teeth against the growing pressure that spread from my chest to push against the bones in my skull.

"No!" Bres strained against his father's hold despite the blade pressed against his throat. "He's going to kill me anyway, Aisling."

Brian stepped in front of me, blocking Bres and his protests from my view. "Listen to him, Aisling. You know what you need to do. We can't let them distract us."

"Time is running out, Ms. O'Meara."

At Bannon's unconcerned warning, I risked a glance up to see that the sliver of light had grown wider. We had minutes at most before the eclipse was over, and with each fractional movement of the moon, I could feel the magic swell. Every cell of my body was filled with it. It strained against my bones, stretched every muscle fibre. I didn't know how much I could take before something snapped.

My split second of distraction cost me. Brian grabbed my wrist in a bruising hold.

"We had a deal," he ground out, no longer masking the anger that flashed in his eyes. "His life isn't worth it. You can't let the Order get their hands on the magic."

I tried to yank my arm back, but his grip was like iron. Anger welled up inside me, mixing with a growing sense of desperation. Without thinking, I reached for my siphoning powers, intending to only use enough to break his hold.

I gasped as the force of the power swirling inside me almost sent me crashing to my knees. A tempest filled my core where my magic normally resided as a source of comfort and reassurance. It was vicious and wild, and absolutely terrifying.

It also held my magic just out of my reach.

But as I sucked in air, trying to regain my equilibrium, something else caught my attention too. Something darker and yet strangely familiar. Dub and Carmen's magic.

Before I could examine it further, Kate appeared at Brian's side. Panic clouded my thoughts and I shook my head, pleading. I couldn't fight both of them, not without my magic.

To my surprise, however, Kate placed a hand on Brian's shoulder. Icicles spread from her fingers and down his arm. Her expression was grim as she met my shocked gaze. "No, but she can't let the Watchers have it either."

She gave me a sad smile. "Bad things done for good reasons are still bad. The Watchers don't get to speak for the magical of our world. None of us have that right."

"Kate. What the hell do you think you're doing?"

Brian spluttered. He tried to yank his arm back but found he was frozen to the spot.

I, however, was able to step back from his grasp.

As he tried again to lunge for me, a large brown wolf stepped up to my side. Pete bared his teeth in warning at Brian. The Watcher wisely didn't protest as Kate pulled him back.

The space between us gave me a chance to breathe, but considering Bannon still held his blade to Bres's throat, that didn't exactly count for much.

Another crash of thunder rattled through my bones and I bit back a groan of pain. Reaching down, I would my fingers into Pete's fur, allowing his sold presence to ground me.

Across the space, I met Bannon's steely, unyielding eyes. He seemed unconcerned by Bres's furtive attempts to break his hold. A trickle of red ran down the side of Bres's throat where the blade had presumably cut him as he struggled. The sight of it sent rage coursing through me.

I was so done with being pushed around by powerful men with over-inflated egos. Kate was right when she said that bad things done for good reasons were still bad, but in this case, I was pretty sure I'd be forgiven.

Delving down deep inside myself once more, I sought out the darkness that now resided there. The shadows burst from me with little effort. Long tendrils of inky blackness reached for Bannon and wrapped around his throat. It took a simple thought from me to make them tighten.

As I'd predicted, he dropped his dagger and his hold on Bres in favour of saving his own worthless life. He clawed at his neck, but there was nothing tangible for his fingers to find purchase on.

I shuddered, remembering what that felt like. But as I watched Bres wrench free from his father's grip with blood staining the collar of his top, any sympathy I had in me disappeared. I squeezed until Bannon's face turned puce and all signs of consciousness left his eyes.

As soon as Bres was free of his father's grip, Teagan grabbed his arm and tugged him towards me. They made it within five feet – and suddenly the triquetra flared a bright white. Skidding to a stop, they reared back, shielding their eyes from the light.

Pain exploded in my head. I dropped the stone from my hand as I covered my ears in a vain attempt to hold my skull together. At my side, Pete whined and pawed at me.

Every nerve in my body was on fire, and it felt like I was being stretched in all directions at once. I huddled in on myself, trying to think past the mounting pressure. I was almost out of time. If I didn't move now, I was dead.

But I couldn't move. I could barely breathe.

Wind whipped up from the glowing lines that surrounded me. It lashed at my skin like razors, and I was driven to my knees once more.

I was dimly aware of Pete's howl as he pressed against me, trying to shield me from the onslaught. The wind turned into a vortex around us, and I caught only blurred glimpses of Teagan and Pete through it. They were once more trying to force their way to our side, their arms up to shield their faces.

A blood-red hue fell over the field as the darkness began to recede. The wind howled, so like a banshee cry that terror froze me to the spot even as it simultaneously felt like I was being crushed from inside and out.

What would happen to my friends if I didn't complete the binding in time? Would they be hurt by the backlash?

I cried out for them to go, to get out of here, but my words were swallowed by the roar of the wind.

Tears burned my eyes and I scrabbled at the ground in a desperate attempt to find the shard of stone. We'd made it this far. I couldn't fail them now. I just couldn't.

An arm wrapped around my waist, bracing me just a blast of wind knocked me sideways. I looked up with a mix of relief and crippling fear to find Teagan had somehow reached my side. Her eyes were still doing that odd flicker between purple and blue, but there was a determined set to her mouth, and the fire that blazed in her eyes was all Teagan.

With my best friend supporting me on one side, and Pete pressing closer on the other, I was able to steady myself enough to rise up on my knees.

A hand reached down to me, and I squinted up through the blinding tears to find Bres in front of me. He grasped my hand and pulled me to my feet. There was something unreadable in his expression as he held an object to me. It took my brain a moment to register the shard of Liath Fáil in his hand. My first instinct was panic.

Had I been a fool to trust him?

Was he going to destroy the artefact so I couldn't bind the magic?

He took my hand and wrapped my fingers around the stone. His blue eyes blazed as he raised his other hand to cup my cheek. "Finish this."

The words had barely passed his lips when a blade of lightning forked through the sky. It struck the ground at the centre of the triquetra. Right where I stood.

CHAPTER THIRTY-TWO

Electric blue light flared all around me and pure, unfiltered agony flowed through my body. I threw my head back and screamed.

The pain was so immense that I couldn't think straight. My hand locked around the piece of stone, but I couldn't form coherent thought, let alone remember what I needed to do with it. Hot tears streamed down my cheeks, and it felt like every part of me was on fire.

"Aisling," Bres yelled, reaching out to grasp my shoulders.

Teagan's panicked cry and Pete's terrifying growl came from each side of me. Whatever was happening to me didn't seem to be affecting them, but the fierce wind lashed at us all, and I could see Bres struggling against it to stay next to me.

"Bres... I... It's too much," I gasped, barely able to speak for the pain.

My vision darkened as my head swam. I couldn't take it much longer.

"Hold on, Aisling. You have to hold on just a bit longer. One final step. That's all."

His words registered with me, but they were distant as a strange numbness settled over my body. Some part of me became untethered just like the magic, and then I was floating.

The world turned white and I was once more back in that place of nothing. Only this time, instead of the calm rainbow current, the magic bubbled around me like a boiling pot on the brink of overflow. I reached a shaking hand out to touch it.

And I shattered.

"Aisling, please, hold on. You have to fight. Please. I've got you."

"We have to get her out of here."

"No. It's too late for that. She has to finish it. Come on, Aisling, you can do this. I believe in you."

The voices, they were so familiar. They surrounded me, cocooning me in a blanket of love and concern, and I reached for them even as I remained unmoored.

Warmth touched my cheeks, and I was shocked to find I still had a physical body capable of feeling such things. The touch called to something deep within my soul, and I focused on it for all I was worth. I used it as an anchor, pulling me back to my body as my cells reformed, one painful piece at a time. Bres's soft words continued, pleading with me, encouraging me every step of the way.

But even as I became aware of my physical self once more, a new pressure grew inside me. It pushed against every limit of my body and soul, stretching, tearing. I was becoming undone at the seams, and even with Bres and my friends at my side, I knew I had seconds at most before nothing would hold me here in this plain of existence.

A defiant roar ripped free of my throat. It wouldn't end like this. *I* wouldn't end like this.

With every last bit of will I possessed, I forced the hand that held the stone to move. I raised it above my head and plunged it down. As it sank into the earth, I screamed the words of binding over and over until my throat was raw and the words were little more than raspy whispers.

Magic flowed from me in an opalescent torrent. My whole body shook violently, but I refused to let go. I willed the magic to find its true place. It belonged to the earth; even if this was my last ever act as Guardian, I would return it there.

In front of me, all I could see were Bres's blue eyes, wide with wonder and fear as he loaned me his strength.

And then I saw the figure behind him.

I couldn't even scream as Bannon rose from the ground like a wraith. He lifted his dagger and plunged it down towards Bres's back.

Black hair whipping around her face and opalescent magic flowing all around her, Teagan stepped forward to intercept the head of the Order. She opened her mouth, and I braced myself for the end that was sure to come for us all with her banshee cry.

Except, it didn't.

A haunting song filled the air, merging with the howling wind. It was sorrowful and beautiful, and it vibrated through my very being.

Bannon jerked to a sudden stop, his blade frozen mid-air.

The banshee's lament rose and rose, sending goosebumps pealing across my skin. And as Bres turned in shock to see what was happening, Bannon's grip released on the dagger, sending it clattering to the ground. He dropped to his knees next to it, hung his head in his hands, and began crying like a baby.

Another sound filled the air, joining in harmony with Teagan's song. The worshipping howl of a wolf to the moon, and I looked up as the moon's shadow disappeared entirely.

Time hung in that one single moment.

Then, on a final exhale, all the strength left my body.

I collapsed bonelessly, but strong arms grabbed me before I could hit the ground. Bres hauled me up, cushioning me in his warm embrace as around us, the wind began to calm and Teagan and Pete's songs faded to the whisper of a memory.

I inhaled deeply as energy flooded my cells. It was vibrant and alive, and all around us. It was life itself.

Even as the heady realisation struck me, the scorched earth that spanned the width of the stone circle began to change. Vivid green tips pushed up through soil that was regaining its colour as nature was rejuvenated by the magic taking root deep within the land. Possibility. That was what Bres had called it. And now the land was filled with it.

A sob wrenched free of my chest, and I buried my face in Bres's shoulder. He held me as my whole body shuddered with the storm of emotion bubbling up inside me. I was alive. We were alive. We'd done it.

Teagan's arms wrapped around us, enveloping us both, and a strong, warm, furred body pressed against my side as Pete joined us in the moment.

I gave myself a minute to get my emotions under control before raising my head to seek out Brian. He stood on the far side of the now-fading triquetra, glaring at us all with barely restrained animosity as Kate still held his arm in a frosty grip.

"I believe that if an officer of the law witnesses an attempted murder, the appropriate steps are for said officer to arrest the perpetrator." I gestured to Bannon, who was still sobbing on the ground even as the final remnants of Teagan's magic drifted away on the air.

Brian's scowl deepened, but he nodded at two Watchers who stood nearby, wide-eyed and noticeably pale. They hurried to cuff Bannon, and something eased inside me as they led him from the stone circle.

I stood there for the longest time, enveloped by my friends as I took in the enormity of what had happened. Against all odds, we'd done it. The magic had been returned to the land, and the people I cared about were alive.

Still, I couldn't help but feel a strange sense of loss mixed with the elation. Our lives had changed with the return of magic, and now that it was back in its entirety, I knew that change would be irrevocable. Whether for better or worse, I wasn't yet sure.

At that thought, I shifted my focus inwards, delving deep inside to examine what lay at my core. The vibration of my magic was stronger now than it ever had been before, even within the pure, unfiltered energy of the dreamscape. It pulsed in sync with my every breath, and I knew with complete certainty that it would come to me with only the merest hint of a thought.

And it wasn't alone any longer either.

The less familiar threads of Dub and Carmen's magic wound through it now, dark and unknown.

Was it evil?

I didn't know.

If it was, then it would be my cross alone to bear. The rest of the magic had been returned to its rightful place in the land. We didn't have to worry about the effects of it being tainted, and I would guard this new magic just like I would the land's. Because even if the magic was out of reach for anyone to Claim, I had no doubt there were plenty more people out there like Bannon who would seek to increase their power.

They believed they had a right to the magic. They were wrong.

Turning around, I moved to the southwest corner of the triquetra and yanked the sword from the ground. I weighed it in my hand, remembering how it felt to wield it in the trials.

"It suits you," Bres said, walking to my side, his hands shoved into the pockets of his jeans.

I smiled, turning the blade over, my eyes taking in every detail. "It might raise a few eyebrows if I go around pretending to be Xena, warrior princess."

"Why don't you test that theory on Friday night?"

A surge of panic quickened my heartrate. Was there another magical apocalypse nobody had told me about?

"I'm letting you take me out for a date," Bres clarified. "You can bring the sword to make sure I behave." He gave me a cheeky wink.

My mouth dropped open. Was he really trying to blag a date at a time like this?

Before I could tell him what to do with his date, his expression softened, turning serious. "You did it, Aisling. Despite everything that was thrown at you. You refused to let them break you."

My cheeks heated and I looked away, unnerved by the intensity of his gaze.

"She'd have liked you, you know. My mam," he clarified at my questioning look. He nodded his head towards Bannon – who was now struggling as two Watchers led him away in handcuffs – and grinned. "I wish she could have been here to see this. To see him like that."

I couldn't help but smile at the sight myself. Still, my heart ached for Bres. "I'm sorry."

He shook his head and turned to take my free hand. "Don't be. You've saved me, Aisling. In ways I can't even begin to put into words. I'll never be able to thank you for that."

We stayed there like that for a long time, watching as what remained of the Order were led away in a similar state to Bannon. The sun shone overhead in a sky so blue it was hard to imagine the storm that had raged not so long ago. When Teagan and Pete joined our side a while later, I hooked my arm through Teagan's and lifted my face to the sky. I let the sun's warmth bathe me ... and imagined I was back in the dreamscape, sitting under its warm sun one last time.

Goodbye, Killian. Thank you.

CHAPTER THIRTY-THREE

O*ne week later*

"Breaking news. Political chaos as head of leading party, the Order, charged with attempted murder just days before the polls open. We bring you more on this news story as it unfolds."

Teagan glanced at the television as she returned from the kitchen with three glasses of wine in hand. She handed one to Pete as she passed the chair he was relaxing in and then the second to me before settling down next to me on the sofa with her own.

"So, they got the charges to stick," she said, indicating to the news reporter who was rehashing the details of Bannon's case on the screen.

"Still time for him to buy his way out of it," Pete muttered, taking a sip of his wine.

I hit *mute* on the remote control, deciding I'd had enough of thinking about Bannon for one evening. We'd been following the news closely for the past week, the three of us gathering in Teagan's apartment to monitor the fallout from the Order's failed Claiming attempt.

At first there was widespread disbelief around the charges Bannon had been levelled with. Somehow he'd become the people's champion, and they were convinced he was being framed in an attempt to discredit him before the election. But as more information came to light, including allegations of bribery and coercion, the narrative had shifted. Now, the Order had skulked back into the shadows, and it looked like Bannon's run for government was at an end.

"How's your mam doing?" Pete asked, shifting his attention from the television screen to me.

I tucked my feet up under me and sighed as I cradled my wine glass. "She's fuming that the police refuse to charge Bannon with kidnapping. Maybe they'd have taken her more seriously if she hadn't tried to paint herself as some Joan Wilder heroine who'd fallen prey to the charms of an evil caricature villain." I shook my head. "The woman didn't even realise she'd been kidnapped until they were strapping her to a damn standing stone."

Teagan chuckled. "Did you explain to her what was going on?"

The three of us had debated for a long time about how much truth was too much when it came to the magic now filling the air around us. Someday, there would be no hiding its existence, but the Watchers did have one thing right – the situation needed to be managed carefully, or we'd all be finding ourselves on the wrong end of a fear-driven witch-hunt. My mam, however, had seen enough that keeping the truth from her seemed pointless.

"I tried. She thinks Granny O'Meara has been filling my head with nonsense and stormed off to give her a piece of her mind."

This time, it was Pete's turn to shake his head in amusement. "She has a phenomenal capacity for blissful ignorance. I almost envy her. My mam is still calling me on a daily basis to make sure I haven't had another breakdown, and I'm pretty certain she thinks I was on drugs. If I'd taken your mam's approach when magic first came back, maybe it wouldn't have taken me so long to accept my wolf."

I gave him a sympathetic smile. "Maybe. Or maybe you'd still be in denial about it now, and I'd be dead multiple times over. I couldn't have done any of this without you guys."

My vision blurred as tears filled my eyes – not for the first time this week.

Teagan scowled and pointed a warning finger at me. "Stop that. No more tears. Drink your wine."

I gave a less than dignified sniff and laughed. "Okay. Okay. How is Jessie doing? Have you been talking to Kate?"

Teagan's eyes brightened with excitement. "I was

speaking to her this morning about some possible venues for the centre. Jessie is staying with her for a while. It's early days still, but now that she's not being treated like a lab rat by the Watchers, she's less afraid of her power. It's a good thing too, because I have a feeling her magic is only going to grow stronger."

I didn't miss the shadows that darkened my friend's eyes at the mention of Jessie's time with the Watchers, and I was sure it was making Teagan re-examine the tests they put her through in a whole new light as well.

As it turned out, that had been what changed Kate's opinions about the Watchers. It was easy to believe that the work they were doing was for a good reason until you had to watch your terrified teenage niece be treated like a science experiment. After stepping in against Brian at the Claiming, she'd disassociated from the Watchers entirely. She and Teagan were now working together to set up a centre that could help train more kids like Jessie to deal with their emerging powers. There was still a lot to figure out – including how to identify new magic users before they freaked out and caused harm to themselves or others – but I had complete faith in my friend to make it work.

"You know I'm happy to lend a hand in whatever way I can."

Teagan flashed me a grateful smile. "I know, but you need to focus on your studies so you can get that law degree."

I grimaced. If there was one thing this whole mess had taught us, it was that we needed to be prepared to stand up to people in a position of power. The best way I knew how to do that was through the law. So, I'd issued the Watchers a politely worded "stuff your job" email and had registered for night classes to become a fully fledged solicitor. It would mean working day and night for a while, but I was determined to make sure that magic users had someone who would be able to stand for them legally when things started to shift.

My phone buzzed on the sofa next to me, and I looked down to see a message from Bres. I couldn't help the smile that tugged at my lips as my belly gave a little flutter of excitement.

Teagan nudged me with her foot. "Have you put him out of his misery and agreed to a date yet?"

My smile widened. "Not yet."

She shook her head, laughing. "The poor guy will have blue –"

A knock on the door cut her off before she could finish what I was sure was going to be a less than lady-like comment. The three of us looked at each other in surprise. We were all here. Who would be at the door, and how did they get past the front door of the building without buzzing up first?

Instinctively, I called my magic to me as Teagan rose from the sofa and made her way to the door. Pete, too, stilled in that unnatural way that warned of the predator lurking beneath the surface.

Teagan pulled open the door, and the tension left her frame a moment before she exclaimed, "Anthea!

What are you doing here? I thought you weren't coming for another week."

An old lady with curly grey hair shuffled past Teagan, holding a gnarled wooden cane in one hand. She gave Teagan an affectionate pat on the cheek before turning to me and Pete with shining blue eyes.

She smiled. "Something told me I might be needed here earlier than expected. Now, why don't you introduce me to your friends."

NOTE FROM THE AUTHOR

Thank you for joining me on this adventure through Ireland's hidden (for now) supernatural world. This is entirely a work of fiction, so while I have taken inspiration from well known Celtic myths, I hope you'll allow me some poetic license with these as I build this new and exciting world.

If you enjoyed this book, I would be very grateful if you could leave a brief review (it can be as short as you like) on the site where you purchased your copy.

As an author, reviews are the most powerful tools in my arsenal when it comes to getting attention for my books. Honest feedback goes a long way in increasing visibility and helping me to reach other readers like you, so thank you in advance!

To get exclusive bonus material and be the first to hear about new releases, promotions, and giveaways **Sign up for my Newsletter at** *https://lmhatchell.com*

ALSO BY L.M. HATCHELL

To see the latest on all my books and upcoming publications,
visit

https://lmhatchell.com/books